"Who are you and how did you get in here?"

Sabrina entered her room. There was a guy standing in front of the mirror that hung from the back of her closet door.

The boy turned. "Oh hi, Sabrina," he said casually. He looked somehow familiar.

"Hey, buddy, you just better tell me what you're doing here right now!" Sabrina told him.

"Don't sweat it, Sabrina. I don't bite . . . anymore." The boy licked the back of his hand, then calmly began washing his face with it.

Sabrina looked at the black hair and the goldish-green catlike eyes. There was an expression in them that she'd seen before. "Omigosh," Sabrina gasped, realizing in an instant that she *did* know this boy, in fact she knew him very well. "Salem. It can't be. Not again! But how did it happen? You were supposed to stay in cat form for a hundred years!"

Salem looked at Sabrina guiltily. "Um . . . the hundred years are up?"

"No chance." Then, in a flash, she understood. "The Heart's Desire chip. Where is it?"

Titles in SABRINA, THE TEENAGE WITCH™
Pocket Books series:

All Pocket Book titles are available by post from:
Book Service By Post, P.O. Box 29, Douglas, Isle of Man IM99 1BQ
Credit cards accepted. Please telephone 01624 675137,
Fax 01624 670923, Internet http://www.bookpost.co.uk
or email: bookshop@enterprise.net for details

While the Cat's Away

Margot Batrae

Based on Characters Appearing in Archie Comics

And based upon the television series
Sabrina, The Teenage Witch
Created for television by Nell Scovell
Developed for television by Jonathan Schmock

POCKET
BOOKS

LONDON · SYDNEY · NEW YORK

POCKET
B O O K S

An imprint of Simon & Schuster UK Ltd
Africa House, 64-78 Kingsway
London WC2B 6AH

A CIP catalogue record for this book is
available from the British Library

ISBN 0 671 02924 X

1 3 5 7 9 10 8 6 4 2

Printed by Caledonian International
Book Manufacturing, Glasgow

This book is dedicated to anyone who has ever taken in a stray, street animal, or shelter pet. You never know—there might be a little warlock in any of them!

While the Cat's Away

Chapter 1

"Salem, get out of there!" Sabrina complained. The jet-black cat curled around her feet, then leaped onto the shelf of the open linen closet, sending a pile of freshly washed towels tumbling to the floor.

"I, Salem Saberhagen, am Supreme Ruler of this linen closet," the cat answered, his goldish-green eyes flashing. He waved a cautionary paw at Sabrina. "And if you don't watch out, I'm going to banish you to the laundry room." Salem yawned then curled up on a heap of sheets, leaving a little swirl of black hair on them.

"Salem, come on. I mean it!" Sabrina swatted the indignant cat off the linen. She had no time for this. She was already risking missing the school bus. But Aunt Hilda liked her to put the towels away by hand. When she used her magic, the green ones always got mixed in with the blue ones.

"Oh, you're no fun," Salem said grumpily, skittering

out of the way. Once a warlock himself, he had made the unfortunate attempt at taking over the world and had been sentenced by the Witches' Council to one hundred years as an ordinary house cat—no magic powers at all other than the ability to talk. It hadn't left him humbler, just bitter.

Sabrina ignored the cat and pointed at the towels. A light dust of sparkles shot out from her finger and swirled around them. They magically refolded themselves and rose into a neat pile on the shelf, though the green and blue ones were all mixed up. They blocked out the dark passage that led into the depths of the closet and far, far beyond. The Spellmans' linen closet had a lot more inside it than pillowcases and extra blankets. It was a doorway to the Other Realm, where most witches lived, away from the mortal world.

Sabrina loved visiting her Aunt Vesta there. You could eat chocolate ice cream for breakfast and no matter what outfit you put on, you never got a panty line. Still, she was glad she and her aunts Hilda and Zelda lived here in normal, mortal Westbridge, Massachusetts, despite homework, zits, and the occasional Saturday night without a date. Besides, when things got to be too much of a drag, she could always simply point . . .

Sabrina was just putting away the last of the washcloths when she felt the first drop. "What was that?" she asked. Something wet plunked down on the top of her head.

"Don't ask me, I'm only the cat," Salem grumbled.

A couple more drops spattered down. Then there was a whirling gust of what felt like wind from the back of the closet and a spray of rain. "Oh no, Salem, it's a hurricane from the Other Realm!" Sabrina shouted.

She tried to push the closet door closed, but the gathering force of the storm was already strong enough to propel it open again. A whoosh of rain flew at her, soaking the front of her "Girls Kick Butt" T-shirt and black hip-hugger jeans. Her syrupy blond hair flew in a million directions. Her pale blue eyes squinted into the closet. The inside of the closet was black with rain and the towels and sheets swirled crazily in the wind.

"Help!" Sabrina called to Salem, who sat out of reach of the raindrops, casually licking his paws.

As much as she pushed, the storm was stronger. She was getting wetter by the second. There was a massive flash of lightning. *Clunk.* Something hit Sabrina hard, knocking her over. With a wild spin, the storm reversed itself, the wind whirled in the opposite direction, and the linen closet door slammed shut with a bang.

Sabrina disentangled herself from whatever was lying on top of her. "Ohhh," she groaned.

The thing the storm had blown in groaned, too. It lifted itself to its knees. Then it stood up.

"Oh no," Sabrina whispered, staring in terror. A man stood there, blinking and dripping all over the floor. Or rather, a warlock. His overgrown black hair had been blown into a tangled mess and his glasses sat askew on the bridge of his nose. He was wearing a very wet white disco suit and a pair of white platform shoes that made him even taller than normal. In his hands were a very wet bunch of flowers and a soggy box of chocolates. He did not look pleased. Salem recognized him, let out a tiny, frightened hiss, then slunk quickly down the hallway and into Sabrina's room.

"Uh-oh, I think I'm in trouble . . ." Sabrina gasped. It was Drell, a powerful member of the Witches' Council and one of the grouchiest warlocks in the Other Realm. Even though the storm hadn't been her fault, she had a feeling somehow she'd end up paying for it.

"Where am I?" Drell muttered to himself. "That interrealm tornado blew me *way* off course." He peered at his watch, put it up to his ear, shook it, listened again, then frowned. "Late! MaryBeth is going to *kill* me." He shook his dark hair, sending a splatter of rain around the Spellmans' hallway. Slowly, his eyes came into focus and settled on Sabrina. His face turned a very delicate pink, then it got red. Finally, it became a deep bluish purple. "Oh no. Don't tell me that storm blew me into Hilda Spellman's house, of all places."

Sabrina chipped a bit of purple nail polish off of one of her fingernails. "Okay," she said, "I won't tell you."

"Of all the unbelievably inconvenient coincidences . . ." Drell muttered at a rattlesnake pace. He stared at Sabrina, looking wet and confused.

"Look, maybe you'll feel better once you get out of those wet and—if you don't mind me saying it—totally outdated clothes," Sabrina said. She nodded her chin at his polyester suit and white ruffled shirt, open to the belly button, out of which peeked a half a dozen gold chains hung with oversized medallions.

Drell looked down at himself, noticing the disco-era outfit for the first time. "Ugh!" he said. "I must have gotten stuck in a 1970s time warp." He pointed at himself and . . . nothing happened. There was only the sound of an engine trying unsuccessfully to turn over. He pointed again. Again nothing. "Shorted out!" he exclaimed.

"What's wrong?" Sabrina asked.

"It's Mother Nature. She's done a whammy on me. She's just never forgiven me for breaking her window playing catch back in the year 1428."

"Look, why don't you get dry the mortal way—with a towel." She pulled on the linen closet door, but it was wedged shut as if glued.

"No use trying that!" Drell said. "It won't open until the inter-realm tornado clears. Besides, open that door in a storm like this one and you could find yourself blown right into the middle of the Salem witch trials."

"Wow! How long can something like that last?" Sabrina asked.

Drell shrugged. "Could be a couple of days, could take years. In any case, we all better get used to sharing washcloths. That linen closet isn't opening any time soon."

"Hey wait. What do you mean, *we?*"

Drell let out a snort of laughter. "What I mean is that you aren't getting any towels and I . . . I'm stuck here until that storm clears." He shook his head mournfully and tried his finger a few more times. The motor-grinding sound went on and on, then finally died completely. He looked devastated. "What a ghastly fate. Stuck in the mortal realm without my powers. They'll laugh me out of the Warlocks' Club if they ever find out about this one!"

"Look on the bright side," Sabrina said, trying to do just that herself. "At least things can't get any worse."

"Sabrina! What's going on up there? There's an awful lot of banging." Aunt Hilda's voice floated up the stairs, followed by the sound of her feet trudging up the stairs.

"It just got worse!" Sabrina and Drell said at the same time.

Drell looked around wildly. He waved his finger frantically at himself. "Got to get out of here. Got to get out of here!" he chanted over and over. But his finger just let out the hissing sound of air escaping from a flat tire.

Sabrina understood Drell's predicament. Drell and Aunt Hilda had a history. They'd dated back in the seventeenth century, or something like that. They'd even planned a wedding, ordered a couple fields of black orchids and brought Homer out of retirement to do the entertainment. But at the last moment, Drell had ditched out, never shown up, left her at the altar. And even though it was all ancient history now, Hilda still hadn't gotten over him. She even sometimes accepted a date with him—though he *still* usually didn't show up.

"Sabrina?" Aunt Hilda called again, this time closer. "Hurry up or you'll be late for school."

Drell stared at Sabrina, desperately reaching out to her. "Help me!" he begged.

"What do you want me to do?" Sabrina asked, shocked.

"At least get me out of these clothes. I can't let Hilda realize my powers are temporarily off."

Sabrina couldn't help having a little compassion for Drell. As clumsy and rude as he could be, it was hard turning down someone who liked you as much as Hilda liked him. On the other hand, Drell had always been a little on the obnoxious side. It felt good to have him momentarily at her mercy.

"Why should I help you instead of my own aunt?" Sabrina asked. She picked a little more polish off her fingers, as if they had all the time in the world and Hilda wasn't about to poke her head up the stairway in a mere few seconds.

Drell's expression shifted. His eyes bulged and his lips trembled. "Please!" he pleaded.

Sabrina watched him nibble his lips anxiously. Actually, it really was a terrible sight. She thought about what it would be like to show up for a date with her boyfriend Harvey and realize at the last moment she'd somehow been zapped into a Marcia Brady outfit. "Okay, okay," she said. "I'll pop you into something a little more presentable. What style and time period do you want?"

"Um, anything's okay," Drell mumbled. "But . . . wait, first, you've got to do me a favor."

"Another favor?"

"Yeah." He fumbled in the pocket of his disco suit, then pulled something out. "Here. Keep this for me." He held whatever it was out. Sabrina opened her hand and he dropped it in. It was a heart-shaped chip that shimmered slightly with all the colors of the rainbow.

"Wowwww!" Sabrina said. It was the most perfect thing she'd ever seen. "What is it?"

Drell frowned, as if he couldn't believe she didn't know. "It's a Heart's Desire chip, of course. Eat it, think of your heart's desire, and it's yours. No limitations, no mess-ups, the way there sometimes are with spells. And it works on anyone—mortals, gnomes, even chipmunks.

Valuable. Very valuable. In fact, nine witches out of ten would rather have that chip"—he pointed at the shimmering heart in Sabrina's hand—"than the power to turn back time!"

"Wowwww," Sabrina said again. "Are you giving it to me?" she asked hopefully.

"No!" Drell made as if to grab the chip back, but Sabrina pulled her hand out of his reach. "I'm just asking you to *hold* it for me while you change my clothes."

"Ohhh," Sabrina groaned in disappointment.

"It's too wet to use right now. But when it dries out, I'm going to use it to whisk myself back to the Other Realm, despite the tornado. If you pop this disco suit back to the seventies with that chip in the pocket, I'm stuck here! And let me tell you, I'd rather watch twenty-four hours straight of *Dance Fever* reruns than be stuck at Hilda Spellman's house, trying to explain why I ran out on her all those centuries ago."

Sabrina barely heard what Drell was saying. What was her heart's desire? To be totally loved by Harvey? She already had that. To travel around the world? She could do that with the point of her finger. To live forever? Witches did. No, she didn't really know what her heart's desire was. Maybe that was part of being a teenager. But it didn't matter. If she didn't have the answer herself, the chip would figure it out for her and then . . . who knew what wonderful things would happen?

"Come on, come on!" Drell's voice interrupted her daydream. "Hilda's coming—you've got to get me out of these clothes!"

"Okay!" Sabrina told Drell. With a fluid gesture, she

started to point, then stopped. "What kind of outfit do you want?"

"Anything! Anything!" Drell practically sobbed as the top of Hilda's head bobbed up the stairs.

Sabrina shrugged and said a little spell. *"Fashion, passion, let it rip. Change this warlock, make him HIP!"* She pointed. There was a little flash of sparkly light. When it cleared, Drell was dry, and he was wearing a pair of messy cutoff jeans and a T-shirt featuring a picture of the lead guitarist of Sabrina's favorite band, the Leopard Spots. A tattoo of a witch on a broom had appeared on one of his forearms and a little silver ring hung from the edge of his right eyebrow. He was still holding the flowers and candy.

Sabrina admired her handiwork. "You look great!" she exclaimed.

"I look ridiculous!" Drell said, scowling.

But at that moment, Hilda bounced up the stairs. When she saw Drell, all energy seemed to drain instantly from her body. Her eyes locked into his and an ocean of emotions washed over her face. Anger, surprise, regret, frustration, and—Sabrina was sorry to see it—love. She was wearing a mud-brown sweatshirt with a dried green glop from an old spell smeared across it. Her blond hair hung mousily around her ears, and she'd neglected to put on her makeup. She was munching on a bagel with cream cheese and a few crumbs clung to her chin.

Sabrina could see her aunt trying to play it cool. "Oh hi, Drell," Aunt Hilda said calmly, as if she didn't care one way or the other whether she ever saw him again. Then she noticed the flowers and candy. A wave of amazement and delight passed over her features. "For me?" Drell looked at her sheepishly, then held them out to her. "Drell! You shouldn't have!" she cooed.

"He didn't," Sabrina said, too quietly for Hilda to hear. A little worm of guilt was beginning to eat at her. After all, Hilda was her aunt. It was already obvious Hilda was going to get her heart broken yet again.

"These flowers are beautiful," Aunt Hilda said, burying her nose in them. "And the chocolates! Hmm, let me give you something, too." She looked down at her half-eaten bagel, pointed, and it turned into a silver breakfast tray filled with a plate of eggs Benedict, pancakes with real maple syrup, fresh orange juice, and coffee with pure cream.

"Uh, thanks," Drell said, not sounding very thankful, though he did take the tray.

"So you just thought you'd *blow by* and see if there was any *splash* left in the old romance?" Hilda giggled.

"Uh, you could say that," Drell said timidly.

Hilda moved in closer. "You really are sweet, you know that?"

Sabrina couldn't stand to watch it any longer. She edged toward the door to her room as Drell shot her a desperate look. Just before she slipped quietly through the door, she turned and pointed at her aunt. The green gunk on the sweatshirt faded away and an unseen hand magically removed the bagel crumbs and brushed Hilda's messy hair. It was the least she could do for her aunt.

Inside her room, Sabrina dropped heavily onto the bed, burying her face in the brightly colored bedspread with an appliqué of the sun on it. Scattered in a jumbled heap on the patterned Persian rug lay a couple of spiral notebooks, along with textbooks, a pair of old gym shorts, Sabrina's history paper on the Great Depression, and a purple felt-tip pen with the cap off. She pointed and the pen capped itself. Then, everything floated easily into her knapsack, ready for the school day. "Omigosh, what have I done?" she asked herself out loud. The purple walls of her room seemed to close in around her.

Drell was standing on the other side of the door looking like a refugee from a grunge concert and Hilda was headed for heartbreak. She sat there, trying to think of some way to get Drell out of Westbridge without turning Aunt Hilda into an emotional basket case. But Drell had already said they couldn't use the linen closet until the storm cleared. They'd just have to wait until the Heart's Desire chip dried and Drell wished himself home.

Her hand went automatically to the pocket of her hiphuggers, where the Heart's Desire chip glowed warmly. She dug in and pulled it out, staring at it in amazement. If only it were hers!

But it wasn't. She shrugged and tossed it carelessly onto the cluttered surface of her desk.

An exasperated voice came floating through the closed door from the hallway. "Sabrina, I think it would be a good idea to get back out here!" Drell called.

Sabrina sighed, rolled off the bed, and hurried out. "Okay, I'm coming, I'm coming," she said as the door swung shut behind her.

For a moment, the room was still. The Heart's Desire chip lay on Sabrina's desk next to a half-eaten chocolate bar and a couple of hair clips. In the soft morning sunlight, it began to glow more brightly.

"Mrreow," Salem purred, slinking out from beneath the bed. He leaped up on the desk and sniffed curiously at the chip. "Wow. A Heart's Desire chip. Neat," he said. He put out his tongue. He licked the chip. Mmmm. It tasted like tuna. He ate it.

For a moment, all was quiet. In the next instant, there was a sound halfway between the blaring of trumpets and a foghorn on a dark night. A pink light surrounded Salem and lifted him an inch or two off the desk and gently enfolded him in its magic.

By the time things cleared, the transformation was complete. Sitting on top of Sabrina's desk, in place of the little black cat, was a slim guy of about seventeen. His tousled black hair just reached the bottoms of his slightly pointy ears. In one of them, a small ruby earring glittered brightly. He wore a sleeveless black T-shirt and faded black jeans. He looked down at himself, his goldish-green eyes flashing with amazement.

"Goodbye dry cat food!" he said. He smiled. Then, very quietly, he started to laugh.

Chapter 2

Sabrina pushed open the door to her room and stopped. There was a guy standing in front of the mirror that hung from the back of her closet door. He kept pointing at his image and muttering to himself. "Who are you and how did you get in here?" she demanded. Cute as he was, she readied her finger to point, in case he turned out to be some kind of weirdo.

The boy turned. "Oh hi, Sabrina," he said casually. He kept on pointing at himself. He looked somehow familiar.

"Hey, buddy, you just better tell me what you're doing here right now!" Sabrina told him.

"Don't sweat it, Sabrina. I don't bite . . . anymore." The boy licked the back of his hand, then calmly began washing his face with it.

Sabrina looked at the black hair and the goldish-green catlike eyes. There was an expression in them that she'd seen before. "Omigosh," she gasped, realizing in an instant that she *did* know this boy; in fact, she knew him very well. "Salem. It can't be. Not again!"

Salem had convinced Sabrina to turn him into human form once already. It had been a huge mess and the Witches' Council had almost ended up throwing her to the lions. Salem had had a great time, however.

"But how did it happen? You were supposed to stay in cat form for a hundred years!" Sabrina moaned.

Salem looked at Sabrina guiltily. "Um . . . the hundred years are up?"

Sabrina shook her head. "I don't think so."

"Maybe the Witches' Council gave me time off for good behavior."

"No chance." Then, in a flash, she understood. "The Heart's Desire chip. Where is it?" She glanced at the spot on the desk where she'd dropped it. "Salem, you ate it!" She let out a moan. "Salem! That was *Drell's* chip." For an instant, she imagined all the horrible things Drell was going to do to her when he found out that chip was gone.

Salem licked his lips and let out a little purr. "Well what did you expect? At the time I did it, I was just a dumb house pet." He pointed at himself one more time, then gave up. "No powers, Sabrina," he said, looking sad. "Even a Heart's Desire chip couldn't give those back to me."

"That's good. What were you trying to do, anyway?"

"Oh, just zap myself into a crown and royal robes. I mean, if I'm going to be Supreme Emperor of Earth, I've got to start dressing the part."

Sabrina rolled her eyes. "I don't know what planet you think you're living on, Salem, but last time I checked, teenagers weren't running the world. Hey, we hardly even run our own lives, or there'd be a lot less homework and detention and a lot more Foosball and pool parties. And speaking of detention, I'm going to get plenty of it if I don't get to school pretty soon."

"Maybe it's not a perfect life," Salem said. "But at least now I can open the tuna-fish cans by myself!"

He looked so excited, so completely happy. Sabrina refused to meet his eyes. She didn't want to be the ants at Salem's picnic, but he was going to have to get turned back. Poor cat. You couldn't blame him for wanting a little more excitement out of life than chasing around after a catnip mouse toy.

But if the Witches' Council found out Salem had gotten turned back into a human, she was in big trouble. They'd probably blame her aunts as well. Hilda and Zelda didn't deserve that—they hadn't even known about Drell or the chip or anything. Besides, Sabrina reminded herself, Salem was being punished by being a cat for a reason. He'd tried to take over the world. And from the looks of things, he still hadn't completely given up on the idea. No, as disappointed as Salem was going to be, she had to turn him back.

"Sorry, Salem, I really am," she said. Very quietly, she began to murmur a spell. *"Magic powers, bring me joy. Salem, you're a cat, not a boy."* She pointed.

Sparkles danced around him. They settled on his hair like fairy dust. Then they turned ashy white and slowly faded away. Salem stood there smiling, flexing and stretching his hands, which hadn't turned back into paws.

Something was wrong with her powers! She threw her

hands up in frustration. As her finger pointed toward the ceiling, a loud explosion erupted and a bit of plaster came tumbling down onto the rug. No, nothing wrong with her powers now. She pointed at Salem a few more times, mumbling spells desperately, but none of them did any good.

"Salem, what's wrong? My powers aren't working on you!"

She didn't really expect an answer from him. He wanted to stay human, so if he knew anything, he sure wasn't going to tell her! Ugh! When her aunts found out about this, they were going to ground her until she was 127 years old!

She rolled over and buried her head under a pillow. It was times like these that she wished she was just a normal teenager, someone who thought witches' spells were just a silly gimmick on a Friday night TV show. Why couldn't she have a regular life with an ordinary mother and father instead of living here in this crazy house with her two magical aunts?

Thinking about her parents, Sabrina sighed. Her mom and dad had split up a few years ago. And while plenty of kids at school came from divorced homes, Sabrina was sure none of their parents had ever had a marriage as crazy as hers had—her father a warlock and her mother a mortal. Sabrina rarely saw her mother, who was an archeologist on some big important dig in Peru, and her relationship was her father was kind of, well, two-dimensional. Still, Dad was probably her best shot at getting out of this mess.

Sabrina hurried to the closet and opened it. She pawed

through a pile of old gym socks, T-shirts, and dirty underwear until she found it—a jewel-encrusted, leather-bound tome called *The Discovery of Magic*. Her dad had given it to her for her sixteenth birthday. Last time she'd talked to him, she'd gotten so annoyed at him that she'd slammed the ancient book closed and tossed it on top of her laundry.

Now, she flipped to the "S" page and sought out her father's name. There he was, Edward Spellman, looking handsome if somewhat old-fashioned with his ebony black hair, carefully combed mustache, and neat evening clothes. The black lines around the photo shimmered, then came to life.

"Hey, Sabrina! Good to see you. You didn't exactly take the time for a gentle goodbye after our last visit," he said. He rubbed his nose.

"I'm really sorry I slammed the book on you, Dad," Sabrina said sincerely. She hated it when she fought with her father. It wasn't really his fault that he didn't understand her. He was stuck between the pages of some old book. It wasn't like he'd ever messed up a big math test or missed a date because a spell went wrong.

"So, sweetheart, what can I do for you?"

Sabrina hedged, trying not to just blurt out her problem. "Oh, nothing really. I wanted to say hi," she lied.

"Aren't you going to be a little late for school?"

Sabrina's smile tightened. "Well, I've missed the school bus, but there's still plenty of time to zap myself over there using molecular transference."

Sabrina's dad smiled at her. "Got a new friend?" He nodded with his chin toward Salem, who waved once, then slunk as far as possible from his curious eyes.

"I guess you could say that," Sabrina said unhappily.

Her father nodded in satisfaction. "Good, honey. I'm glad. A nice young warlock. You know, I worry about you sometimes, spending all your time with mortals. I wouldn't want to see you get into a situation like your mother and I did . . ." There was a sad, faraway expression in his eyes as he said it.

Sabrina wanted to soothe him, make that expression disappear from his face. But she didn't have the time right now, she realized, as she noticed Salem staring out the window very intently. The sky was blue and clear. It was hard to believe that just on the other side of the linen closet, a terrible storm was raging. But Salem wasn't looking at the weather. A robin was chirping on the window ledge. Salem swallowed hard, looking hungry. Very, very slowly and very, very quietly, he lifted the window. Then, he lunged for the bird, managing to snag a few tail feathers as it fluttered out of reach.

"Uh, Dad, have you ever heard of something called a Heart's Desire chip?" Sabrina asked, trying to sound casual.

"Oh, sure! Those are so great!" He closed his eyes as if remembering far into the past. "I had one back in 1776. Boy, was that a terrific year! Declaration of Independence, American Revolution, George Washington, and all that. Sometimes I think that Heart's Desire chip I ate may have had a little something to do with how things turned out back them, you know what I mean?"

He winked. Then he said, "Why do you ask, Sabrina? Don't tell me you've actually gotten your hands on one!" He looked really excited.

Sabrina sighed. "Well, not exactly. The thing is, Dad, I wondered . . . well, is there any way to reverse the chip? You know, turn something back?"

Sabrina's father laughed. "Why would anyone want to do a silly thing like that?"

Sabrina shook her head. "I didn't mean your own heart's desire, I meant someone else's."

Her father nodded. "Oh, now I get it. But no, honey, I'm afraid there's no magic strong enough to reverse another person's heart's desire, unless of course they don't want it anymore."

Sabrina let out a low moan. "Dad, no! You've got to be wrong!"

He shook his head, making the border around his picture wobble slightly. "That's the amazing thing about a Heart's Desire chip. Once you get what you really want, no one can take it away from you."

"You're kidding! Then I'm stuck with things the way they are?"

"I'm afraid so." Sabrina's father looked out of the book, studying her face hard. "What's the matter, sweetheart? You aren't in any kind of trouble, are you?"

"No, of course not," she said. By the window, Salem was motioning wildly at the bird, which fluttered just out of reach. "Hey! Cut that out!" Sabrina shouted. Salem looked up and the bird, startled by the sound, flew to the top of the tree.

From the hallway, Drell's voice called out, blocking

out the sound of Salem's frustrated exclamations. "Sabrina!" he shouted. "Get out here pronto!"

"Sabrina, are you sure you're okay?" her father asked. "Maybe I should have a talk with one of your aunts."

"Sabrina!" Hilda's voice called from the hallway. "Hurry up and go to school! Or do I have to come in and get you?"

Sabrina stared at Salem. She mustn't let her aunt see him. "No, Aunt Hilda! I'm coming!"

"Sabrina! Flip me over to Hilda," her father insisted.

"Sorry Dad, gotta go!" she said. She slammed the book shut.

"Oww!" she heard her father complain from between the closed pages.

At that moment, the door of the bedroom swung open. "Aunt Hilda!" Sabrina exclaimed. She tossed the book back in with the laundry before her aunt could see it. She stared around, feeling caught, just in time to see Salem's jeans-clad rear end disappearing out the window and crawling onto the branch of the tree. He might fall, but at least he was out of sight.

"Young lady!" Hilda scolded. "If you think I don't know that you're already"— she looked at her wristwatch, a tiny sundial on a gold wristband—"two and a half minutes late for school?" But she was obviously in too good a mood to stay mad. Without her knowing it, her scowl transformed into a grin. "Oh, Sabrina, I'm so happy! Drell has decided to stay with us for a few days." She whirled around the room, giggling. "I think he's finally realized that he loves me! After all the time I've dreamed of this, it's like having my heart's desire come true!"

Sabrina groaned, too stunned to say a word.

Hilda stopped and locked eyes with Sabrina. "Now I want you to make him feel comfortable here. *Very* comfortable. When he asks for something, you give it to him."

"Don't worry, Aunt Hilda. I would have had to do that anyway," Sabrina said in a faint voice.

"Good, well I'm glad we're tuned to the same radio station on this point." She whirled out of the room, grinning blissfully.

Sabrina ran to the window. "Salem? Salem!" she called out. There was a rustling in the green leaves of the tree, but she couldn't catch a glimpse of a person. Behind her, the door flew open a second time. It was Drell.

"How could you do this to me?" he wailed, pointing to the Leopard Spots T-shirt and the eyebrow piercing. "Now your aunt thinks I'm into this stuff. She's even whipping up a pair of backstage passes to a Rumpelstiltskin concert over at the Westbridge Coliseum!"

"Go! You'll have a great time," Sabrina said.

Drell glared. "It's my greatest heart's desire that you get me out of this ridiculous outfit. Now!"

Sabrina pointed. The T-shirt went poof, the pants disappeared. Drell stood there in nothing but a pair of Mickey Mouse boxer shorts. "Ooops! Sorry," she said. She quickly pointed again. This time, she popped him into a pair of huge elephant-leg pants and some platform sneakers. His T-shirt said "Python! The World Tour."

"Cool! You're into Python? They're terrific!" Sabrina said. Drell scowled. "What's the matter? You're totally styling!" Sabrina said, admiring her work.

But Drell wasn't looking at his clothes. He was staring past Sabrina's shoulder. Out the window. Into the tree.

Sabrina turned. *Uh-oh,* she thought. Salem was climbing over the windowsill, a few red feathers sticking out of his mouth. Thinking fast, she came up with the first fib she could think of. "Drell, meet my boyfriend. His name is . . . um . . . Solomon."

Drell pinned her with a sharp stare. "Solomon, shmolomon! There's a shifty look in those eyes I'll *never* forget. Salem Saberhagen. Former warlock. Wannabe world ruler. And until very recently, a common house cat." He turned toward Salem. "Salem, you're looking a lot better than the last time I saw you. Or should I say, a lot more *human.*"

"Must have been that self-improvement course I took," Salem said. "Amazing, the changes you can make with positive thinking."

Drell didn't answer him. He pointed his chin in Sabrina's direction. "Explain this to me," he said. "Please, tell me I'm dreaming."

Sabrina chewed on her nail, trying to think of something to say, but the only thing that came to mind was the truth. "Maybe you *are* dreaming. Maybe this is your heart's desire and it just came true . . ."

A look of understanding, then disbelief passed over Drell's face. "He ate the chip. Salem ate *my* Heart's Desire chip. Which I gave to *you* for safekeeping. Now I know I'm dreaming. Sabrina, this is a nightmare!" He hitched up his huge pants, looking small and helpless.

"I'll make it better, Drell, I promise. I'll get Salem turned back!" Sabrina cried.

But he just sighed and looked miserable. "Gone. My Heart's Desire chip is gone forever." Shaking his head, he turned on the heels of his high-topped sneakers and slumped out of the room.

"Nice pants," Salem commented.

Sabrina rolled her eyes. She paced around her room in a little circle, nibbling off some of her purple nail polish. She was in an impossible situation and, to make it worse, she was already incredibly late to her first-period chemistry class. But as hard as she thought, no answers came to mind. She was stuck with Salem as a teenager—at least for now.

"Come on," she said to Salem.

"Where are we going?"

"School, where else? If I stay here one more second, I'm going to lose my mind. Besides, I've got to get to class."

Salem let out a little yowl. "Hey, I spent the last time I was a human being at Westbridge High and, believe me, once is enough. That Mr. Kraft—what a nightmare! Besides, I'm not enrolled there as a student. Go yourself. I'll just stay home and watch kitty commercials on television."

Sabrina shook her head. "Uh-uh. Leave you lazing around here making trouble all day and there's no telling how low Drell will zap me on the evolutionary chain when he gets his powers back. Also, one of my aunts is sure to disrespect the boundaries of my personal space and barge into my room. If they find you here, I'm toast."

"Why don't you just do a molecular transference spell and send us both to Disney World?"

"Nope. You're a teenager now, Salem, and what teenagers do is go to school."

Salem mewed unhappily. "But I'll be bored! And besides, I'm meant for better things! Why do I have to go to high school when I ought to be out there taking over the world?"

"You'll have plenty of time for that after college," Sabrina said easily. Then she pointed, and they were gone.

Chapter 3

Sabrina and Salem popped into the school broom closet just as the second bell was ringing. Outside the door, they could hear kids talking, lockers slamming, feet hurrying down the hall. Above it all, Vice Principal Kraft's voice wailed like a siren. "Get to class, or the whole school's staying for detention this afternoon!"

Darn! Sabrina thought, scrunching up among the mops, pails, and bottles of floor polish. After the crummy morning she'd had, all she needed was for Mr. Kraft to catch her in here. She was uncomfortably aware of Salem beside her. He was perched on what would have been his hind legs, listening carefully, his nose twitching.

"Salem, stop it!" Sabrina whispered. "You're human now. You can't act like a cat."

"Ooops, sorry," he said. "Old habits." He straightened up, banging his head against a shelf of toilet scrub. Half a dozen bottles of the stuff started to tumble. Sabrina pointed at one, two, three, four, five bottles. They hung for a moment in the air, then floated back onto the shelf. She missed the sixth, though, which crashed to the floor and shattered.

"Darn!" Sabrina said, staring at the goopy mess. She pointed and it disappeared.

But now the door of the broom closet swung open and Mr. Kraft stood there, huge and furious, peering through his wire-rimmed glasses, his white mustache twitching.

"Hey, I remember you from the last time!" Salem exclaimed, staring into the vice principal's face.

Mr. Kraft ignored him. "Sabrina Spellman! What are you doing in here?" He turned toward Salem and a knowing glimmer came into his eyes. "Oh, I get it. A girl. A boy. A broom closet." He winked. Then his expression turned stormy again. "But if you think I'm some kind of mushy-hearted romantic who's going to let you off detention for sentimental reasons, you've got another think coming!" He started marking Sabrina's name down on one of the red detention slips he always had clipped to his Student Demerits notebook.

Sabrina stared first at the vice principal, then at the teenaged boy who, until this morning, had been a cat. "You think I . . . and Salem . . . ?!?" It was the weirdest thought ever. She realized now, as she took in Salem's trim, athletic form, sharp yet delicate features, and glittering goldish-green eyes that in fact he was kind of cute—if you could get over how pointy his ears were. Until this moment, she hadn't really been able to see him as anything other than a kind of overgrown cat standing on his hind legs.

Still, the thought of her and Salem . . . it was too disgusting, like kissing your own brother. Or worse, your cat! "It's not like that, Mr. Kraft! It's not what you think."

"Oh really?" Mr. Kraft skewered Sabrina with a glare. "Well, what *are* you two doing in the broom closet?"

Sabrina peeled some of her nail polish off with her teeth. "Just . . . had the sudden urge to clean up?" She suggested hopefully.

"Okay, then you can clean up at detention! And if you're not in class within half a minute, you'll be cleaning up at detention tomorrow, too. Both of you!"

"But I'm not enrolled as a student here," Salem said coolly, picking a bit of cat hair out from under one of his nails.

Mr. Kraft glared. "No problem. Sabrina will do her detention and yours, too."

"But Mr. Kraft . . ." Sabrina protested lamely.

"I refuse to discuss it," he said. He handed her a detention slip and slammed out of the broom closet.

"Salem! See what you've done?" Sabrina wailed.

"Hey, it wasn't me who popped us into the broom closet!"

"Stupid cat," she muttered, pushing open the door. Outside, the hall had turned quiet. Sabrina motioned him out with her hand. "Come on. We've got to get to chemistry."

But Salem held back, hiding among the cleaning products. "Sabrina . . ." he said.

Even though she was risking more days of detention with every second they were late, there was such a melancholy tone in his voice that she turned. He was staring at her with big eyes and, yes, she could barely believe it but . . . Salem was trembling! "What's the matter?" she asked, amazed that anything could rattle him.

"I . . . I'm scared!"

Sabrina studied this boy who had, until this morning, been her pet cat. He'd always acted as though he knew it all. "You? Who told me you didn't want to go to school so you could stay home and take over the world? You're afraid of a little chemistry class at Westbridge High?"

"I know, I know." Salem tried to wave it off. "But you've got to realize, last time I was a teenager at this school, I was inhabiting a real teenager's body."

"But, Salem. It was *Gordie* you were inhabiting."

Salem waved his hand. "I know, I know. But see, that's just it. No one ever paid too much attention to Gordie. This time, I'm the new kid. And everyone will be looking at me." He shivered. "Except for that one time, it's been *decades* since I've gone out in anything other than a flea collar." Sabrina started to laugh, then cut herself off as she saw the fear in his eyes. "I mean, what if I'm not wearing the right clothes? What if I make a fool out of myself? What if . . ." He was having a hard time getting the words out. "Sabrina, what if I don't fit in?" As if to prove that he never could, he twisted around with the most amazing agility Sabrina had ever seen and started licking his own back.

Sabrina sighed. Salem had gotten her into more trouble this morning than she wanted to think about. Maybe' it would serve him right if he got a little normal teenage embarrassment before she managed to turn him back into a cat.

On the other hand, she had been there herself just a few years ago—nervous, new and a little on the odd side. A tiny thread of pity went out from Sabrina's heart to Salem's. After all, this was *Salem* she was talking about. Her little kitty, who curled up at the foot of her bed and kept her feet warm on winter nights or licked her hand when he wanted to get petted. The fact was, she *loved* Salem. She couldn't just let him sink on his first day at Westbridge High.

Besides, if Salem acted like a real geek, it could rub off on her. After all, she'd brought him. Not only would he ruin his own reputation, he could totally spoil hers, too.

Sabrina made her decision. They were in enough trouble as it was at home. Might as well keep things smooth and comfortable at school. She'd help Salem. She had to—for both their sakes.

"Look, Salem, I'm not going to lie to you," Sabrina said. "The first day is hard. The impression you make today . . . well, it's important. If people decide you're a freak, they're going to make your life miserable."

"So what do I need to do?" He looked terrified.

Sabrina shook her head sadly. "Unfortunately, there's no magic formula. All I can say is don't chase any mice or scratch behind your ears."

Salem listened but he didn't look particularly reassured. "Wouldn't it be easier if we just went home?"

Sabrina thought about it. A million things could go wrong here at school—Mr. Kraft could hassle them again, Salem could make total fools of both of them and

Sabrina's social life could be ruined for months. But then she considered what her aunts would do when they figured out just who the boy with the black hair was—and what the Witches' Council was going to do to all of them when *it* figured out who that boy was.

"No!" she said. "You're a teenager now. You're just going to have to learn to live with school, like the rest of us. Besides, I'll be with you." She threw him a smile. "Come on, now, Salem. Haven't I always taken care of you?"

Salem held Sabrina's gaze for a long, emotional moment. In the silence of the broom closet, Sabrina knew he was imagining countless cleanings of his litter box, fish sticks slipped under the table, and hour-long sessions with the cat brush. He swallowed hard. "I guess you have," he said.

"You ready?" she asked.

"As ready as I'll ever be!" Salem pasted a bold smile on his face as they stepped out of the broom closet and headed for class.

Behind her back, Sabrina crossed her fingers. This just *had* to go well!

As they shuffled out of chemistry forty-five minutes later with the bell ringing in their ears, Sabrina wasn't crossing her fingers anymore. Salem had been terrific! She peeked over at him in awe. He was calmly washing his nose with the back of one of his hands. "Salem," she whispered urgently, "cut that out!"

He looked up with a wounded expression. Then he realized what he'd been doing. "Oh, I'm really sorry!"

He pulled his hand away quickly, but he couldn't resist one last swipe with his tongue around his lips. "I guess I really blew it, huh? You'll probably never be able to show your face in that class again, right?"

"Blew it?" Sabrina said, shocked. He had no idea how good he'd been!

"See? I knew it! I've lost the touch! I've been a cat for too long!" he moaned softly.

"No. No, Salem. You were . . . you were incredible!"

She'd started to introduce him to her teacher and the class as her cousin, visiting from Detroit. He'd cut in, saying he lived in Beverly Hills, which of course had sounded much better. But the really great part had been the rhymes he'd done of the periodic table. "Hydrogen's the first of the elements that we've got. It tends to blow up when it gets hot!" The teacher had looked alarmed at first, but as Salem had gotten into the lesser known elements—"Hafnium's number seventy-two. It's toxic metal so keep it away from you"—the teacher had started to stare at him as if the ghost of Albert Einstein had just made an appearance on MTV. Sabrina had heard her mumble, "It's like my heart's desire has finally come true—a kid who cares about molecules!"

Sabrina had seen how impressed the kids had been. Harvey had started giggling. Even Libby Chessler hadn't been able to keep herself from smiling. Gordie had looked most impressed of all. Of course, he had a special bond with Salem, even though he didn't know it. Salem had actually inhabited Gordie's body for a few days the last time he'd been turned into a human.

Yup, Salem had impressed them all. How could he not have! He'd rattled off all 106 elements with a rhyme for each one. Maybe it was because he'd had so much practice with spells, which rhymed, too. But he hadn't cast a spell in ages! It must be like riding a bicycle—you never forgot how to do it.

The only really hairy part of class had been when Harvey had passed her a note. In his familiar scrawl, it had said, "Why does your cousin have the same name as your cat? Is it sort of like when you had that cat named Sabrina at your house?" Of course, Sabrina had been that cat herself, temporarily turned into a feline by accident. Anyway, she'd passed a note back saying, No, no, nothing like that. It was just that Salem the teenager had actually been the one to give her Salem the cat as a kitten, so she'd named one after the other. It was lame, but it had been all she'd been able to think of.

"So . . . I didn't embarrass you or anything?" Salem asked Sabrina. Around them, people pushed past, their feet echoing on the tiles as they hurried down the hall to their second-period classes. Others hastily undid lockers, their fingers flying through the combinations.

"No way! I was . . . I was proud of you!"

He looked at her with big eyes—exactly the same expression he used on her when she got out the Cheez-n-Baco kitty treats. "You mean it?" he asked.

"Of course I do! You were great!" Sabrina realized it was true. In the eyes of the other kids in the chemistry class, she had the neatest cousin ever. Salem might actually bring up her status at school—if he could curb the instinct to groom himself in public.

"All right!" Salem launched himself into the air in a joyous leap, then landed, catlike, without a sound.

"Wow," Sabrina heard a guy behind them say. "That guy should definitely go out for basketball this year!"

Salem threw her a relieved, proud, slightly silly grin. Sabrina grinned back. Salem seemed to have a real knack for making people like him. It was hard to believe that just this morning, he'd been lapping his breakfast out of a plastic bowl on the floor. He fit in so well! To be honest, she was actually having fun! Well why not? This was Salem, after all, her little kitty pal, the one who purred like a little electric motor every time she chucked him under the chin. In the end, when she got him turned back into a cat, she might actually look back on this crazy day fondly. Because, of course, she *had* to get him turned back. But how? How?

There was no time to think about that now, as the sound of the bell announcing second period went spinning through the halls. She ushered Salem into French class. If he did half as well here as he had in chemistry, she had nothing to worry about. Of course, the real test would come three periods later. No, it wouldn't be a test. It was more like a midterm or a final. Even worse than that, it would be like . . . like the college boards of social acceptance. Just three more periods. Three more periods and then . . . lunchtime!

Chapter 4

U gh, what is that horrible smell?" Sabrina asked Salem and Harvey. A heavy burned odor hung like a dark cloud over the tables of chattering kids. Some of them forked something gray off soggy paper plates, but most of them had found something other than the school lunch to eat that day.

"Who knows *what* the kitchen people have thought up this time!" Harvey groaned. He slid his arm around her waist and gave her a quick, possessive squeeze. He had slipped himself between Salem and Sabrina somewhere between fourth-period class and the doors of the lunchroom. She wasn't entirely sure, but she thought maybe he was jealous. Jealous! Jealous of Salem! If only he knew the truth!

Salem put his nose in the air and sniffed in a decidedly catlike manner. Sabrina stiffened. She wished she could remind him he was human, but there was no way with Harvey squished between them. "Smells like chicken liver dinner to me," he said.

"Liver! I wouldn't even make a freshman eat that stuff!" Harvey exclaimed. "I'm glad I brought lunch today." He held up a brown paper bag with the top rolled up.

Salem sniffed again, this time in the direction of Harvey's bag. "You're kidding! You'd rather eat that than liver?" he said, his catlike eyes wide with amazement.

"Salem!" Sabrina hissed. Then she turned to Harvey and smiled sweetly. "He is such a kidder!" she said.

Now that she thought about it, Sabrina wished she'd brought lunch, too. No day was a good day for liver. But after everything that had happened this morning, she'd totally forgotten to make something.

Without being obvious, she pointed and thought, *Newts and eels and things that whiz. Make our lunches just like his.* She put her hands behind her back and two bags exactly like Harvey's appeared in them. She handed one to Salem. "What'd you bring?" she asked her boyfriend.

"A peanut butter and pickle sandwich," he said. "And a six-pack of Yodels."

"Ohhh," Sabrina said, swallowing a look of distaste. "What a coincidence. So did we!"

Salem made a face. "Well, I guess I'll take my chances with the kitchen people." He waved his paper lunch bag in Harvey's direction. "Hey, you want mine?"

Harvey looked at Salem with surprise and pleasure. "Sure, dude!" He took the bag. But as Salem turned and headed off for the lunch line, Harvey murmured, "Weird!"

Fifteen minutes later, Sabrina saw Salem looking for them over the heads of the other kids. She motioned him over to their table, which had filled up with a few of their friends. He squeezed his way between the orange plastic chairs, ducking a flying bun and just avoiding slipping on a piece of banana peel. His plate was full and he'd lined up about ten half-pint cartons of milk along the rim of his brown plastic tray. He slid the tray onto the table and dropped into a seat between Harvey and Val, who was already halfway through her cheese and tomato sandwich. Next to her, Julie Jarkowitz was shaking the last chocolate chip crumbs from out of a plastic bag and Nathan Milestone was downing a bologna sub.

When Salem sat down, Val hastily put down her sandwich and anxiously wiped away a few imaginary crumbs from her mouth. "Salem! That love poem you recited from memory in French class was *amazing!*" she gushed.

It was true. Salem had been incredibly passionate and suave, especially during the part about *"Le chat, le chat, qui mange le rat!"* Their French teacher had wanted to give him an A right then, even though he wasn't officially a student! Of course Madame DuPlessey would never know that before he'd tried to take over the world and gotten turned into a cat, Salem had spent some time as a count in the court of Louis XIV. Even though he was rusty, his accent was pretty good. Still, Sabrina couldn't believe how Val was staring at him like a lovesick kitten, her eyes all big and liquid.

"Oh, it was no big deal," Salem said. He dug into the liver, shoveling big, messy forkfuls into his mouth. Even then, Val didn't look the slightest bit disgusted.

Oh boy! Sabrina thought. *My best friend's got a crush on my cat!* She had to break the moment. She grabbed one of the milk cartons off Salem's tray and opened it, then handed it to Val. "Hey, did you know most teenagers don't get enough calcium? We're not building enough bone mass and when we turn, like, sixty or something, we're all going to look like the Hunchback of Notre Dame." She pushed the milk into Val's hand. Her friend didn't look like she wanted it, but at least she broke off mooning at Salem.

"Hey, that's mine!" Salem said, snatching the carton out of Val's grip. He drained it in one gulp. Salem took another carton and another after that and sucked the contents down.

"Wow!" Harvey exclaimed, giving Salem a weird look. "What's with all the milk?"

Sabrina looked around wildly, hoping an explanation would appear in her head as if by magic. "He's just . . ."

"Bulking up for football season," Salem finished smoothly. He opened another milk and made it disappear. Sabrina just hoped he digested it before she figured out how to turn him back into feline form and she was once again responsible for cleaning out his litter box. Milk gave cats the runs.

"No way! You play?" Harvey said. He looked at Salem dubiously. "You're . . . kind of small."

A catlike grin slid across Salem's face. "Yeah, but I'm *fast.*"

"And you should see him jump!" Sabrina put in.

"Did you see the Detroit-Atlanta game Monday night?" Harvey asked. He looked a little suspicious, as if he didn't think Salem would have.

But Sabrina remembered seeing Salem curled up in front of the TV watching some kind of sports thing. "Great game! Great game!" he said. "I'm a real Lions fan."

"They just *ate up* the Falcons," Harvey commented.

"You can say that again!" Salem dug into the disgusting mound of brown mush on his plate as he and Harvey headed into a heated play-by-play re-creation of the game. Sabrina tuned them out. Which gave her plenty of time to think about her *real* problem. What was she going to do about getting things back to normal—if you could call having a talking cat who'd once been a warlock normal. She sighed and unwrapped her peanut butter and pickle sandwich. She poked at the pickles, then pointed and they disappeared. As she ate, her father's words echoed in her mind: *"I'm afraid there's no magic strong enough to reverse another person's heart's desire. . . ."*

Sabrina refused to accept it. There *had* to be some way out of this mess. She knew she needed help. The problem was, who could she turn to? If Aunt Hilda and Aunt Zelda found out what was going on, they would ground her well into the next century. If Aunt Vesta had been around, Sabrina could have gotten her advice. But she was off on a three-week package tour of the solar system. Besides, there was no way of getting in touch with her until the inter-realm hurricane cleared—and when it did, Drell would have his powers back. He'd be ticked off about losing that Heart's Desire chip, about getting stuck at the Spellmans' house, about a lot of things. She just had to fix everything before then. She sighed. Things just couldn't be as hopeless as they looked.

Sabrina finished off the last bite of her sandwich. She looked over at Salem. He was laughing and motioning wildly as he and Harvey talked. "Look, the Falcons may be a better team," he was saying, "but they've got no spirit. Now the Lions, that's a team with *teeth*." He bared his own teeth and let out a little growl.

Harvey was listening, nodding, and looking a little mesmerized. "I never thought of it that way, but you're right!"

"Of course I am!" Salem said. "I'm always right."

Sabrina rolled her eyes. He might not look very much like the little ball of black fur he'd been, but it was the same old conceited Salem. He continued miming passes, talking wildly, meanwhile shoving fork after fork of liver into his mouth. Harvey nodded excitedly, eating up every word. Well, at least the guys had figured out something they had in common. And Harvey wasn't looking at her with that jealous scowl anymore. She watched as Salem reached out to throw yet another pass. His arm stretched longer and longer until . . .

"Owww!" someone behind him said as his hand made contact with a head.

Everyone at the table turned. Libby Chessler was standing there in a skirt just slightly longer than her green and white, micro-mini cheerleader's uniform and a pink angora sweater. Her shiny dark hair spilled out over her shoulders. Her usual smirk was firmly lodged across her face, which she was holding as if Salem had just hauled off and punched her. Beside her were her two best friends, Cee Cee and Jill. Whatever nasty thing Libby said, those two were always around to back her up.

"Hey, I'm sorry," Salem said casually to Libby, then turned back to Harvey.

But Libby just stood there, glaring furiously. Great. If Salem so much as twitched a whisker wrong, she'd get half the school whispering about what a loser he was. She had to make Libby go away. If only she could point . . . But of course, with everyone watching, she couldn't. Libby stood there as if she were made of concrete.

"Uh, Salem, this is Libby."

Salem turned back. "Oh sure. Libby. I remember you from the last time I was . . ." Sabrina kicked him under the table to keep him from saying he'd ever been at Westbridge High before. "I mean . . . Sure, Sabrina's told me all about you!" He turned and gave Sabrina a dirty look for kicking him.

"So this is your freaky cousin everyone's talking about," Libby said, sneering. "I mean, he *must* be a freak if he's related to you!"

"Yeah!" Jill said.

"Freakazoid!" Cee Cee muttered.

Sabrina shook her head and sighed. "Libby, why do you always have to act like you have termites gnawing on your brain?"

Libby ignored her and turned her attention to Salem. "So, are you a freak or aren't you?" she asked.

Salem calmly opened yet another carton of milk and drained it, then tossed the box on the growing pile of empties on his tray. "Well, I *have* had a sort of unusual life," he admitted. "If that makes me a freak, okay."

Libby rolled her eyes. "It's no fun if you say it's true yourself!"

Sabrina couldn't stand it. Salem had no idea what he was up against. She was sure there hadn't been anyone as horrible as Libby when he'd gone to high school the last time, which had probably been somewhere around the sixteenth century.

This was exactly the kind of thing Sabrina had promised to protect him from when they'd had that heart-to-heart in the broom closet this morning. She couldn't let him down now. Besides, if he teed Libby off, it was Sabrina who'd have to pay for it all year long. She had to do something!

She couldn't help herself—she pointed. As she did, she thought, *This conversation's real depressin'. Give this girl a little lesson!*

Danny Kramer stood up and sent a large spoonful of mashed potatoes flying through the air. It spun across the room and landed with a plop on Lloyd Krumley's table. "Food fight!" Donovan Stein shouted. In the next instant, buns started to sail. The air was thick with orange peels and empty juice cartons. Libby, standing in the middle of the room, was getting it from both sides. "Yuck!" she shouted, ducking. But it was too late. A piece of liver with her name on it was already soaring across the lunchroom. It collided with her head with a splat. "Ewww," she shrieked.

Sabrina giggled, pointed again, and the food fight faded into a memory.

"Omigosh, omigosh!" Libby moaned as she combed the liver out of her hair with her fingers.

"Ugh. You're a mess, Libby," Jill said helpfully. "And . . . everyone's looking at you!" she added in a stage whisper.

"Really!" Cee Cee agreed. "It's my heart's desire *never* to be in as embarrassing a situation as you are right now."

Libby's face turned a bright, embarrassed purple. With the gravy dribbling down her hair and into her sweater, Sabrina almost felt sorry for her. But not for long. Because now Libby stopped whining and stared around the lunchroom with the furious sneer all of Westbridge High had learned to fear. "Who threw that liver? Come on now! Someone threw it and . . . no one is leaving this room until I know who!"

A cold terror swept the room. Everyone in the lunchroom stopped, forks halfway to mouths, words stuck in their throats. When Libby got in a mood like this, no one was safe. Everyone looked around, but the lunchroom was dead silent.

Then, somebody laughed. It wasn't a mean laugh. It was just relaxed, easygoing. And, Sabrina realized to her amazement and horror, the person making that sound was . . . Salem. *Oh no,* she thought. *Now Libby's going to totally hammer him.*

But Salem didn't give her a chance. "Look, it's only a

little liver." Then he stood up and whisked a comb out of his back pocket.

Before Libby had a chance to react, Salem swept the comb through her hair, gathering it into a neat ponytail. A few twists of his wrist and it stayed there, tied up stylishly without any barrettes. It was almost like magic. And, as Sabrina studied Libby, she realized she didn't look bad. Not bad at all. Sabrina remembered now that back in the eighteenth century, Salem had been a hairdresser in Pittsburgh.

"See? No big deal," Salem said. His goldish-green eyes gazed into Libby's. "Liver's good for the hair, anyway, makes it shine." He sat down again and went back to his meal as if nothing had happened.

And now, the entire lunchroom waited. What would Libby do? She could slam Salem just as easily as she could thank him . . .

Libby just stood there for one moment, then two. She dug in her bag and pulled out a mini makeup kit with a mirror. She held it up and studied herself in it, peering as if she were looking at the Mona Lisa. And then . . . she smiled! Libby turned toward Salem and she actually smiled! "Not bad," she said.

"Of course not. After all, you're dealing with Salem Saberhagen," Salem said.

Libby continued to check herself out. At last, she closed the makeup kit with a snap and slid it back into her bag. "You know, you may be Sabrina Spellman's cousin," she said to Salem, "but you're okay!"

A few moments of shocked silence hung over the lunchroom. Then, the kids broke into chatter. Like the rest of them, Sabrina stared at Salem in amazement. First he'd won over the teachers, then Val, then Harvey. And now, in less than one day at school, he'd managed to do something she couldn't in all the years she'd been going to this school.

He'd won over Libby!

Chapter 5

☆

☆

Sabrina trudged up the concrete walkway to the big old Victorian house she called home. It hadn't been a bad day, except for the detention. That's when Sabrina had had to send Salem out into the big, bad world all by himself. She'd tried to take him with her to detention, but Ms. Quick, who had been in charge of detention that day, had said, "This is not a social club, Sabrina," and she'd pointed Salem toward the door.

Salem had waved to her through the dirty windows of the classroom as he'd left the school building. He'd said he'd go right home, climbing up the ivy vines at the back of the house and in her window to avoid bumping into Aunt Hilda or Aunt Zelda. At the last moment, Sabrina had played it safe. She'd pointed at his retreating figure and popped him into her room. He was probably curled up on the bed at this very moment. Just like in the old days.

Yeah, it had been a pretty good day. Salem had done a great job of keeping those cat impulses under control, except for when they'd passed those cages of mice in the biology lab. Other than that, he'd done fine.

Better than fine. By the end of the day, he'd already finished a history essay it was probably going to take her a week to get through. Though of course, it was easier to write about the Great Depression when you'd actually lived through it. He hadn't said a word when Randy Johnson had copied off his advanced algebra quiz, either. He seemed to understand the rule against snitching by instinct. Of course, Salem didn't have to do any of these things because he wasn't enrolled at Westbridge. He chose to do them. *Just to show off,* Sabrina thought.

But that wasn't all. During the practice football game in gym, Salem had caught so many passes that the coach was already pushing paperwork through to let him play on the varsity team without being enrolled at Westbridge. He was talking about joining the school newspaper staff. And he'd even gotten on Mr. Kraft's good side by cleaning some mucky stuff out of the speakers of the public address system. The Vice Principal's announcements had been especially crisp all afternoon.

Sabrina was proud of him. He was a one-person whirlwind, taking Westbridge high by storm. But . . . she dug in her bag for her keys, not wanting to admit to herself about the other feeling she was experiencing. Jealousy. Just a twinge. This was her school, her life, and, well, Salem just seemed to be doing a lot better at it than she was!

She pushed the thought to the back of her mind. Let

Salem enjoy the little time he had as a human being. He'd be a cat again soon enough. Anyway, she hoped he would be. She wondered how long the inter-realm hurricane was going to hold out. She didn't want to think about what would happen if it cleared and he was still human. Right now, the Witches' Council didn't know about any of this. But Drell was a big tattletale and once he went back to the Other Realm and told everything, Sabrina would be in big trouble. And not just Sabrina, but her aunts, too.

Sabrina found her keys in the bottom of her knapsack. They jingled as she unlocked the front door and pushed it open. As she stepped inside, she could already hear Drell's deep voice floating in from the kitchen. "These crab cakes are a little dry, Hilda," he was saying. He sounded tired and, worse yet, deeply annoyed.

"But sweetie pie, I made them myself!" Hilda answered.

"Oh, that explains it," Sabrina heard Drell say.

Pushing back dread, Sabrina walked into the living room and dropped her knapsack on the couch. "I'm home!" she called out.

"Sabrina!" came a chorus of voices from the kitchen.

She heard footsteps and in a moment, three bodies appeared in the doorway. Drell was still in the Python T-shirt and elephant-legged pants she'd pointed him into this morning, with the addition of a little white bib that said, "Maryland is for crabs" in red letters. Behind him, Hilda was dressed in a slinky evening gown that showed every buxom curve of her body and her blond hair was brushed into a sophisticated chignon bun. She held a greasy spatula in one hand, and there was a blissed-out expression spread across her face.

And then there was Zelda, who looked as tired as if she'd just flown round-trip from Boston to China and back again on a broken vacuum. She rolled her eyes behind Hilda's back and made a face. Hilda and Drell must be driving her crazy.

"Uh . . . hi guys," Sabrina said. She was already starting to feel sick.

"Hi yourself!" Drell snapped. He mouthed words at her, *Get me out of these clothes!*

Meanwhile, Hilda was saying, "Sabrina, Drell says he's staying for dinner! Do you think you could pop yourself over to Maine and pick up a half a dozen incredibly perfect lobsters?"

"Don't bother getting any for me," Zelda said, walking over to the couch and dropping exhaustedly into it. "I'd rather go out for Chinese food!"

"Me too!" Sabrina agreed. She didn't want to stick around here and watch Drell and Aunt Hilda drive each other crazy.

"Oh goody!" Hilda said. "Then it'll just be you and me, dumpling," she said to Drell, giving him a little half hug from behind. "It's like having my heart's desire come true!"

"Come to think of it, I wouldn't mind a little Chinese," Drell muttered, easing out of her embrace.

"Come on, muffin! The frog legs ought to be just about ready," Hilda said. She grabbed Drell by the arm and dragged him back into the kitchen. As they left, Drell turned over his shoulder and mouthed at Sabrina,

My clothes! She pointed. Drell's pants and shirt shifted around his big frame. In the next instant, he was wearing Hawaiian print shorts and a T-shirt that said, "My grandparents went to the Caribbean and all I got was this lousy shirt." He glanced down at himself, frowned, and shook his fist in Sabrina's direction. In the next instant, the kitchen door swung shut behind him.

When they were gone, Zelda closed her eyes, groaned, and fell onto the pillows of the couch. "Ohhhh, Sabrina, it's been awful! Hilda's just throwing herself at that warlock and he . . . well, I can't really figure out why he's here. He clearly hates it, but he doesn't use his powers to pop himself out of here. And every time I edge him in the direction of the linen closet, he just looks at it as if it's a stairway to the dead zone. Maybe he's here on some kind of dare, or a punishment from the Witches' Council. But then I keep wondering, what did *we* do to deserve *him?*"

"Yeah, pretty weird," Sabrina said. Well, at least Drell hadn't decided to make her life ten million times worse by telling everything to her aunts. Every hour he spent here was a danger to her. Yet the moment the inter-realm hurricane cleared and he got his powers back, the Witches' Council would hear everything and then she would *really* be in trouble. "By the way, have you heard a weather report?" she asked.

"Oh sure. The guy on the news said to expect more sunshine and crisp, autumn afternoons," Zelda said. "Don't you hope this weather keeps up forever?"

"Yeah, sure," Sabrina answered gloomily. If only it would! She got up and headed for the kitchen. Maybe she could get an Other Realm weather report on the toaster.

"Hey, have you seen Salem?" Aunt Zelda asked as Sabrina pushed through the kitchen door. "He hasn't been around all day."

Sabrina stifled a groan. "Maybe he's hiding from Drell and Hilda," she suggested.

"Well, he isn't a *stupid* cat," Zelda agreed.

"No, he's certainly not a stupid *cat*," Sabrina said.

Sabrina let the kitchen door swing shut. Inside, the wood-framed portrait of Aunt Louisa stared grimly down from the wall at an ugly sight. Aunt Hilda had pulled out what looked like every ingredient in the closets and was mixing things together madly at the counter. She hummed as she worked. Drell was sitting at the table, stuffing his face. There was already a spot of melted butter on the T-shirt Sabrina had zapped him into. Luckily, his mouth was too full for him to say anything to her, because just the way he was looking at her was making her quake in her boots.

"Hey, I'm just whipping up another batch of frog legs," Hilda said to Sabrina, waving her spatula at a mess of stuff frying on one of the burners. "You want some?"

"Uh, no," Sabrina answered. She hurried over to the toaster, fiddled with the dials, then pushed the eject button. A small white card popped out.

The high pressure front continues to sit over the Doldrum Mountain range, blocking access between the Other Realm and the mortal world. Though why any self-respecting witch would want to go there, we're not really sure. But anyway, folks, that inter-realm storm isn't going anywhere for at least the next four days . . .

Whew, Sabrina thought. At least she had a little reprieve. Though having Drell stuck here might kill her just as surely as sending him back would.

"Is that a weather report?" Drell asked sharply. He pushed himself away from the table and snatched the little white card out of Sabrina's hand with his greasy fingers. He read it, scowling. "Don't worry. The weatherman is *always* wrong," he said meanly.

And of course, he was right. Sabrina remembered the time she'd gone to visit Aunt Vesta for a weekend of sailing and beaching and they'd ended up spending the whole time playing Trivial Pursuit, The Witches' Edition in the basement.

"Try some deep-fried worms, pumpkin," Hilda said to Drell. "They're a delicacy in Botswana!" She threw something Sabrina didn't even want to think about in yet another frying pan.

Sabrina wasn't sure how much more of this she could stand. She fled from the kitchen, toward her room. She had to talk to Salem. If he could see what was going on here, he'd take pity on her, wouldn't he? He'd let himself be turned back into a cat, right?

"Sabrina!" Drell roared as she left. Without even looking back at him, she pointed him into another outfit. "Awwgh," she heard him yell as she dashed through the living room and up the stairs, taking them two at a time.

"Salem?" she called out softly as she stepped inside her room and slammed the door shut.

"Salem!" she said again, this time a bit desperately, because there was no one in the room.

"Salem!" Sabrina cried a third time, alarmed now. Her eyes swept the room wildly. But there was no black-haired teenage boy anywhere—not on her bed, not at her desk, not sprawled out on the floor. Under the bed! That's where he must be. That was always his favorite place for an afternoon nap.

She pulled up the edges of the bedspread and stuck her head under the bed. But there was nothing there except a few dust bunnies and a green sock she'd thought she'd lost in the wash.

"Okay, you can come out of the closet now," she said, throwing open the door. Inside, her own dresses seemed to mock her.

Where was Salem? He had disappeared!

Chapter 6

☆

☆

Sabrina lay on her bed, biting her fingernails into little stubs. She'd long since finished nibbling the polish off them. *Oh no, oh no, oh no!* she moaned to herself. Salem was somewhere out there in the big, bad world. Alone. Vulnerable. He'd done so well at school, she'd actually started thinking about him as if he were human. But he wasn't. He was a cat! A cute little kitty. And not just any cat, this was *Salem,* her furry pal who sat in her lap as she did her homework and followed her around the house when she was doing chores. If anything happened to him, she'd never forgive herself. Never!

Of course, if Salem had still been in cat form, she would have told her aunts, combed the neighborhood for him, checked the pound. But what did you do when a teenaged guy was missing—especially one who wasn't supposed to be a teenager at all?

It wasn't until an hour later that Sabrina heard something rustling in the vines outside her window and then a faint tapping on the glass. She looked over to see Salem's catlike eyes gleaming at her from the other side of the pane.

"Salem!" she said furiously. She jumped off the bed and pulled open the window. "Where were you?"

Salem slipped into the room, landing without a sound. "Oh hey, Sabrina. I was bored sitting here alone so I decided to head over to the Slicery."

Sabrina looked at him in amazement for what felt like the one hundredth time today. "You were at the Slicery?"

"Oh, don't worry. I went down the vines. Your aunts never even knew I was there."

"Salem! That's not the point! I was worried about you! You shouldn't be out alone."

He let out a little laugh, halfway between a meow and a giggle. "I wasn't alone. Harvey was there, and a whole bunch of other people."

"You were with Harvey?" Sabrina said incredulously. "While I was doing detention and then watching Aunt Hilda and Drell turn the kitchen into a Julia Child rerun?"

Salem waved his hand in the air, as if that could make all Sabrina's worrying disappear. "It was no big deal. All we did was eat an anchovy pizza."

Images of Salem licking the anchovies right off the pizza pushed their way into Sabrina's head. If he'd done anything totally embarrassing like that, she'd kill him. "What else did you do?"

"We played a little Foosball. Harvey and I make a great doubles team. We slammed everyone we took on."

"Great!" Sabrina said, feeling jealous.

"A few of the guys from the Ridgefield football team were there. One of them called the Westbridge team a bunch of vegetables and, well, one thing led to another. Harvey challenged them to a football game after school on Thursday. I'm going to play for Westbridge. It's going to be terrific!"

"Yeah, terrific," Sabrina muttered.

"Oh, and Val was there. She asked me if I'd go to the movies with her on Friday night."

"That's nice," Sabrina lied. She had the feeling Val's family's car was going to get a very flat tire sometime Friday afternoon. Val might be desperate for a date, but there was no way Sabrina was going to let her go out with a cat, even a very good-looking one like Salem. Besides, Sabrina was beginning to think Salem was having altogether too much fun. She wouldn't have minded nearly as much if she'd been having some herself.

"And Libby asked me to tutor her in chemistry. She heard about my rhyming. She's going to pay me seven dollars an hour."

"I can see you two getting a whole lot of studying done," Sabrina said sarcastically.

"Anyway, she's having a party on Saturday—Libby, I mean. She invited me. Harvey's going, too. And I told her that I wouldn't tutor her unless she invited Val, also."

"Val!" Sabrina exploded. "What about me?"

A confused expression slid across Salem's face. He jumped onto the bed, curled up, and started licking his hands in a most annoying way. "You? You're always telling me how much you hate Libby. I figured you wouldn't want to go."

"I would if all my friends were!" Sabrina said. "Or better yet, maybe anyone who *says* they're my friend should boycott that stupid party. I mean, why would you *want* to go to Libby's, anyway?"

"Maybe because there's gonna be great food there, a keg of real root beer, live music by Venus and the Fly Traps . . ."

"Okay, okay," Sabrina said. "You've made your point."

"So . . . what are you going to be doing Saturday night?" Salem asked innocently.

Sabrina started a slow burn. Well, she'd hoped she and Harvey could head up to the Point or something and do what everyone did there—make out. But there was no chance of that now. And there was no one else to spend Saturday night with, either. Even Val would be busy. "Probably the same thing you are, *cat*. Curling up with a good book in bed! Or should I say, *under* the bed, which is where you'll be."

Salem cocked his head to the side just the way he did when he was a cat. He looked at her, hurt. "Oh, come on. You wouldn't really want me to miss that party, would you?"

Sabrina let out a sigh. "Salem, Salem, Salem. How could you possibly go? You might do something . . . cat-like. Then you'd ruin your reputation forever."

Salem scowled. "Please! What do you take me for?"

"Well, you know, you really are a cat, Salem. A cat! And the sooner you get back to being one, the better."

Salem stared at Sabrina, his goldish-green, almond-shaped eyes blinking in amazement. "You're kidding, right?"

Sabrina shook her head. "I've never been more serious in my life."

Now Salem opened his mouth and a huge belly laugh–like yowl came out. "That's a good one. Really! Because you know, I was just about to say that your Heart's Desire chip was the best thing that ever happened to me. I *love* being human and more than that, I love being a teenager. I'm *never* gonna change."

"Oh yes you are!" Sabrina countered. "You better! Or else . . . or else . . . or else, Salem, my life is *over*. Totally over. There's no telling what the Witches' Council will do to me."

Salem wiped away a nonexistent tear. "That would be so sad. But I know you'll figure some way out of it."

Sabrina stared at him, shocked. "You mean you . . . you don't care?

Salem sighed. "I'm sorry, I really wish there was room for me to worry about your problems. But when you're trying to take over the world, some of the little people have to be sacrificed." He made a sweeping gesture with his hand, as if he could just brush Sabrina's whole life away without a thought.

"Take over the world? All I've seen you do is take over my friends, my classes, my life!"

Salem shook his head sadly, as if he had compassion for Sabrina, but the moment didn't last. "That's the first step. First your life. Then Westbridge High. Finally, the world!" He spun around the room as if it were a tiny globe and he was its master.

Sabrina crossed her arms over her chest and snorted. "That's funny. That's really funny. Taking over my high school is supposed to be a first step to taking over the world?"

Salem turned back to her, looking surprised. "Hey, lots of politicians got their start in student government."

"But you're not on the student government at Westbridge!" Sabrina pointed out.

Salem smiled confidently. "Oh, I will be. Libby and I talked about it at the Slicery. She suggested I run as her vice president."

"You and *Libby?*" Sabrina said, incredulous.

"Uh-huh," Salem said, standing in front of the mirror and admiring himself. "But I convinced her we'd sweep the election if *she* were *my* vice president." He turned his attention to Sabrina again. "We can count on your vote, can't we?"

Sabrina threw herself on the bed in disgust. "Salem! How can you be president of Westbridge? You aren't even a student there!"

"Libby said we could convince Mr. Kraft to make an exception."

Sabrina buried her head in her hands. Libby was probably right. "But the elections aren't even happening for, like, six months or something."

"We're getting an early start on our campaign," Salem said smugly. "It'll be easy to win. After that, I plan to get elected president of my class in college, too. When I graduate, I'll become a Senator's aide, then a Senator myself. Pretty soon, I'll be leader of the Western world!" he explained. "I'll have the best army on the planet at my disposal. The FBI, the CIA. Hey, I'll even have NASA. We'll send rockets up and take over the universe!"

"No, no, no!" Sabrina moaned. She picked up a pillow and held it over her head to avoid hearing more. It was all happening so fast. And when Salem talked about it, it seemed so horribly doable. She wondered if they served Pretty Kitty Treats at the White House.

"You see how it is," Salem went on, gently now.

"Oh, I see all right!" Sabrina said. He had to be stopped. Someone had to teach this kitty a lesson, and fast. Even if he didn't succeed in taking over the world, he was certainly making a mess of *her* world.

"I'm glad you understand. It's all for the best," Salem said, his pointy ears twitching. "And I'm sorry if my plans cause any chaos in your tiny, insignificant life." He gave Sabrina a comradely pat on the back. "Gotta go now," he said, turning back toward the open window. "The football team's having a barbecue tonight and they invited me as an honorary member."

"Salem!" Sabrina bounced off the bed, grabbed his arm, and spun him around. "You are not going anywhere! At least not until I figure out how to turn you back. You *are* getting turned back, you know."

Salem pulled out of Sabrina's grip. "Who are you fooling?" he said. "You know as well as I do that there's no way to reverse someone's heart's desire. I'm human. I *want* to be human. And I'm going to *stay* that way."

Sabrina shook Salem. "No, I refuse to believe it," she wailed. "There's got to be a way to change you back.

Drell wants you that way. And not just him. It's the whole Witches' Council and . . . and . . . and me, too."

Salem studied Sabrina seriously. He sat down on the bed and folded his hands one over the other. "Sabrina, don't you understand?" he said earnestly. "I *like* drinking twelve cartons of milk for lunch. I *like* being popular at school. I *like* acing all the tests and doing great in class. And I'm going to stay this way. For the rest of my life."

"It can't be. It just can't be," Sabrina wailed.

"Now maybe it's time we broke the news to your aunts."

"No!" Sabrina shouted.

Salem sighed. "Sabrina, Sabrina. You're merely putting off the inevitable."

"No, I'm not," she said, knowing what he said was true.

"Now look," he said. "I'm going to this barbecue. I'm going to have a great time and fill my stomach with as much steak as I can. You're going to stay here and have a little heart-to-heart with Hilda and Zelda." He leaped off the bed and headed for the window again, his behind swishing back and forth as if it were a tail. He slung first one, and then the other leg over the sill. Just before he grabbed the vines and shimmied down, he turned back. "And by the way," he said, "when I come back, I'm taking the front door, like any normal human being."

"How could you be normal? You're a cat, Salem, a *cat!"* Sabrina shouted helplessly after his disappearing form.

But he didn't hear. Or at least he pretended not to.

Chapter 7

Sabrina crept down the stairs, hoping her aunts and Drell wouldn't still be in the kitchen. She had to talk to someone and Aunt Louisa was the only one she could think of for now. She peeked into the living room. Aunt Hilda and Drell were zoning out, watching a videotape of *The Wizard of Oz*. Drell was wearing a pair of black leather pants, a Killer T-shirt, and a pointy goatee. Hilda had changed into a low-cut gold number with sequins and spangles around the plunging neckline. She was snuggled up in the crook of Drell's arm and he was busy shoving handfuls of W&Ws, the Other Realm version of M&Ms, into his mouth. The light shone in from Aunt Zelda's study. Sabrina could hear her whipping something up on the laptop. Good, the kitchen would be empty.

"Hi!" Sabrina said to Aunt Hilda and Drell as she passed through the living room. She tried to sound casual.

"Hi," they said without looking up. She headed for the kitchen.

The place was a mess. The pan Aunt Hilda had used for the frogs legs was in the sink. Aunt Zelda hadn't even closed up the containers of leftover Chinese food and put them in the refrigerator. Her aunts had probably had one of their arguments about whose turn it was to clean up. It was all so stupid when all you had to do was point. Sabrina did. The water started splashing into the sink and the pans magically cleaned themselves. The tops of the Chinese food cartons folded themselves up and the food popped itself into the refrigerator. The trash grew two tiny legs and ran itself out to the garbage shed.

"Thank goodness *somebody* cleaned up!" a voice called out.

Sabrina looked up at the portrait of her Aunt Louisa, which covered up the secret spice cabinet where her aunts kept their witch ingredients. Her stern face stared out of the picture frame in disgust. Every hair in her tight bun was in place. The lace collar of her black dress was clasped with a cameo pin at her throat.

"If they don't care about a clean kitchen, you'd think they'd respect *me* enough to throw out the trash. But *noooooo!*" the portrait said, shaking her head.

"Aunt Louisa!" Sabrina exclaimed happily. "I was just coming to talk to you!"

Aunt Louisa's severe expression softened. "What's the matter, child? Something's wrong?"

Sabrina pulled one of the kitchen chairs out from the table, turned it around and sat down in it backwards. She rested her arms on the top of the chair back and her chin on the backs of her hands. She let out a deep sigh. "Aunt Louisa . . . I'm in trouble."

Aunt Louisa looked down at her gently. "Tell me about it. I'm all ears." A few extra ears sprouted up and down her neck, then faded away.

"See, it started with Salem . . . I mean, it started with Drell . . . I mean, well, there was this Heart's Desire chip. Drell gave it to me until it dried out. And then I left it on my desk. And then, see . . . Salem ate it!"

"He did? Well that explains why he didn't eat his lunch." Aunt Louisa nodded with her chin toward the full cat dish. "So . . . what did he wish for? A lifetime supply of tuna dinners?"

"No!" a voice from the doorway said. "Salem wouldn't waste a Heart's Desire chip on something so insignificant."

As Sabrina turned, a little bubble of nausea ballooned in her stomach. Aunt Hilda was standing in the doorway, a stunned expression on her face, the empty candy dish of W&Ws in her hand. She'd obviously come to fill it back up. And she'd heard . . . everything.

"So come on. Tell us what he wished for." She looked steadily at Sabrina, not blinking. Sabrina swallowed hard but the words wouldn't come. "Okay then, *I'll* tell you," Aunt Hilda said. *"He wished to be human.* Didn't he? Of course he did! That's the only thing Salem's ever wanted!"

Sabrina stared at the floor, avoiding Aunt Hilda's eyes. "I'm sorry," she said humbly. "It was an accident. It wasn't my fault."

Aunt Hilda stood there, her hands on her hips. "Oh Sabrina! Don't you know what the Witches' Council will do to us if we don't get Salem turned back?"

"What?" Sabrina asked.

Aunt Hilda waved her hands in the air as if she'd swallowed something nasty. "I don't exactly know. And I *definitely* don't want to find out." Her expression shifted to nervousness now. "Uh, Drell doesn't know about this, does he?"

The door of the kitchen swung open again. "Of course I know!" Drell was standing there, his bulky body filling the door frame.

Aunt Hilda turned to face him. Sabrina could see her thinking, putting all the pieces of the puzzle together one by one. A devastated look of rejection washed across her features. Sabrina's heart went out to her. "Then . . . then you came here because of Salem, not because of me?"

Drell shook his head. "Of course not!"

"Really?" Aunt Hilda looked so hopeful. Sabrina couldn't stand it. Drell treated Aunt Hilda like some kind of Other Realm dish towel—if the Other Realm had had dish towels (witches didn't do house chores, they just pointed). "Then you *did* come here to see me!" Aunt Hilda exclaimed.

"Well, uh . . . I wouldn't exactly say that . . ." Drell hedged.

Hilda glared at him suspiciously. "Then what would you say, exactly?"

Drell shuffled his feet sheepishly. "There was an inter-realm hurricane and I got blown here by accident."

"Oh," Aunt Hilda said, sounding miserable. Her lower lip trembled.

Don't cry! Sabrina wanted to shout at her. *Just don't let him see you cry!*

She didn't need to say it. Right in front of their eyes, Hilda seemed to pull herself together. Anger zinged through her, giving her a little glow.

"Now I understand everything," Hilda said softly. "The clothes that just weren't you—Sabrina did that to you, didn't she?" Drell nodded. "Poor baby," Aunt Hilda said, eyeing his leather pants and goatee. "Let me fix that for you."

"Thank goodness!" Drell breathed a sigh of relief. "Hilda, I'll never forget you for this."

"You bet you won't!" Aunt Hilda said. She pointed. A little puff of smoke came out of her finger and enveloped Drell. When it cleared, he was wearing a pair of polyester bowling pants and a T-shirt that said "I love Barry Manilow."

"Hilda!" Drell gasped, amazed.

"Want a snack, Drell? Here!" Hilda pointed and a burned meatloaf appeared on the kitchen table. Then she pointed at herself and turned her glittery gown into an old pair of sweatpants and a T-shirt she'd probably used to paint the garage back in 1950 something. She called into the other room. "Zelda, we've got a little problem. I'm calling a family meeting." She pushed open the kitchen doors and beckoned Sabrina after her with her finger. Drell started to follow her into the living room. "Not you!" she said. "I said a *family* meeting and you are definitely not family." She pushed through the door and let it slam closed in Drell's face.

Good going! Sabrina thought. She was glad her aunt was done moaning over Drell. She followed Aunt Hilda into the living room. Aunt Zelda was just walking in from her study. She settled into the couch, looking up at Aunt Hilda expectantly. "So? What's up?" she asked.

Aunt Hilda dropped into an armchair and explained everything in a no-nonsense tone of voice. Never once did her voice tremble or a tear escape her steely eyes to let on that she was, at this very moment, suffering a broken heart. She must realize that Drell was probably listening to every word, his ear pressed up against the crack in the door. When Hilda was done, the two aunts turned to Sabrina.

"Do you think Salem will be willing to turn himself over to the Witches' Council, like he did the last time he got turned into a human being?"

Sabrina shook her head. "No way. He just told me what a great time he's been having. And that he's planning to stay this way forever."

Hilda and Zelda both let out a huge sigh. "Then we'll have to figure out another way to turn Salem back," Aunt Zelda said. "For the good of all of us."

"Not just us," Sabrina admitted uncomfortably. She refused to look at either aunt.

"What do you mean?" Aunt Hilda asked.

"Salem may be a human now, but he hasn't changed a bit." With her teeth, Sabrina ripped away the last bit of her final nail. "He—he's still trying to take over the world."

Aunt Hilda buried her head in her hands and moaned. "Noooo. Just like the last time he got turned human. You see? That's why the Witches' Council turned Salem into a cat in the first place. We were supposed to make sure he stayed that way! And now, this is the second time we've messed up.

"Sabrina, do you know what the Witches' Council does to people who fail a direct order?"

"Turns them into termites!" Drell called from the kitchen.

Hilda shot a dirty look at the door, then went on. "So now, it's up to *you*, Sabrina Spellman, to make sure Salem gets turned back."

"Or you'll all be eating wood!" Drell called again.

Sabrina and her aunts did their best to ignore him. "But I thought there wasn't a way to do that," Sabrina said. She'd been careless with Drell's Heart's Desire chip and now, not only was she going to pay, but so were her aunts and maybe all of the world.

"Sabrina! Would I tell you to turn Salem back if there was no way to do it?"

Sabrina looked up, meeting her aunt's eyes for the first time. "You mean it? We're not stuck with Salem as a human?" Maybe her father had been wrong. Maybe there was a way to turn Salem back after all!

Her aunts looked at each other. "It's not easy but . . ."

"All you have to do is convince the person who ate the chip that whatever they wished for . . ."

"Isn't their heart's desire anymore!"

Sabrina thought back to her father's words again. *"There's no magic strong enough to reverse another person's heart's desire, unless of course they don't want it anymore."* He'd given her the answer right from the start. She just realized it!

"I can't believe it! That's great news. Terrific news!" Then, her voice trailed off as she thought back to how Salem had enjoyed being with Libby after every mean thing that girl had ever said to her. How he'd played up to Val. How he'd practically started spending more time with Harvey than she did. How he was starting to take over the newspaper, the football team. How he'd sucked up to Mr. Kraft. Salem was having the time of his life . . . and he didn't care if everything he did was ruining her life.

Aunt Zelda snapped her fingers in front of Sabrina's eyes. "Earth to Sabrina. Do you understand what we just told you?"

Sabrina nodded. All she had to do was convince Salem he didn't want to be human anymore. Make Salem wish he weren't human . . . The impossibility of that task slowly began to sink in. "But I'll never be able to do that!" she protested. "I've never heard Salem wish for anything other than to be human. And now, he thinks he's going to be president, or emperor, or something like that!"

"Then you better come up with a brilliant way to make him unhappy!" Aunt Zelda suggested.

She pulled her feet up under her and caressed the bitten ends of her nails, thinking hard. How could she possibly convince Salem that a cat's life was ever so much

better than a teenager's? Complicate his romantic life?
Steal his notes before the big science test? Remove the
elastic waistband of his uniform just before he ran onto
the football field?

Hmmm, she thought. *This is going to be fun!*

Salem knew something was wrong the moment he
pushed open the front door. As he stepped inside, no one
gasped, no one exclaimed, no one even looked his way.
Sabrina, Zelda, Hilda, and Drell all lay sprawled on the
couch or curled up in armchairs. On the TV screen,
Dorothy from *The Wizard of Oz* was just launching into
her big speech. "If I ever go searching for my heart's
desire, I won't look any further than my own back yard,"
she said.

"I'm back. Did you miss me?" Salem said, scanning
their faces for some sign of reaction.

"Not really," Sabrina said. "How was the barbecue?"

"Great," he answered, his ears twitching suspiciously.
They knew. Sabrina had told them and they'd come up
with some plan to turn him back.

"Pull up a chair and watch the movie with us?" Hilda
invited.

"Uh, maybe some other time," he replied.

"Homework to do?" Zelda asked. "Better get it done.
And don't stay up too late. It's a school night."

"Hey, why don't you take these W&Ws up for a study
snack," Drell suggested, holding out the bowl.

Salem took it, sniffing it. It didn't *smell* like there was
some kind of potion in it that would reverse the Heart's
Desire chip.

Anyway, there was no way, absolutely no way, he was going to let them do that. He *loved* being human. More than that, he had big plans. Westbridge, Washington, the world! It was going to be all too easy. He didn't know who these Spellmans thought they were, but they would be the forgotten ones of history. He, he would be the one who created the face of the future!

And a couple of witches who didn't have anything better to do on a Wednesday night than watch videos were not going to stop him! Of that, Salem Saberhagen was absolutely certain.

Chapter 8

Mr. Rathbone dropped the last pop quiz onto Gordie's desk, turned to face the rest of the class, and said, "Okay. You can begin."

Students fumbled in desks for pens, snapped their gum, or shuffled the papers around on their desks before confronting the first question. Gradually, the shuffling stopped as everyone got to work. Sabrina picked up her pen with dread. There was no way she could pass this test. She'd barely skimmed the chapter on the Great Depression in the history book last night. She'd been too busy thinking up incredibly embarrassing things to do to Salem to make him want to be a cat again.

She'd even dreamed about it, imagining that she'd pointed Salem into high-waisted polyester pants and a white button-down shirt with egg stains on it just before he'd gotten up in front of the entire school at assembly to make a school election campaign pitch. "It is my heart's desire to be the president of this school!" he'd begun. The kids had laughed him off the stage! Poor Salem. She'd felt sorry for him in that dream.

The important thing now, though, was that she was about to flunk. She, Sabrina Spellman, who always, *always* got A's! She peeked over at Salem. He was happily scrawling away on his quiz. And Randy Johnson was copying every answer onto his own paper. To make matters worse, Sabrina knew that Salem was taking this stupid test of his own free will. Just to impress the teacher. He still wasn't enrolled here.

She stared miserably at the test. *Question 1: Who were the President and Vice President during the stock market crash of 1929?* Vice President? No one ever remembered the Vice President! *Question 2: Name five of the President's responses to the crash.* The words swam before her eyes. She didn't have a clue.

Sabrina struggled through the next forty-five minutes, resisting the urge to peek at Salem's paper herself. He hadn't had to study to know this stuff. He'd lived through it. And his self-confident smile told her he was acing the test.

Well, there were worse things in life than doing poorly on one little history quiz. Getting called up in front of the Witches' Council for high treason was one of them. If she messed up today, she'd have to work twice has hard before the next quiz in order to bring up her grade. But if she didn't get Salem to wish he were a cat again, she'd end up getting turned into an ant or a jellyfish or something by the Witches' Council. And it wasn't only her own life that was on the line, but Aunt Hilda's and Aunt Zelda's, too.

Sabrina muddled through the test as best she could. She got an answer here or there, but there were a lot of blank spaces. She was done long before Mr. Rathbone said, "Okay class, put down your pens." She'd spent most of the class staring out the window, watching the clouds, or staring at the election posters Salem and Libby had plastered all over the walls of the classroom, or thinking about how awful it was going to feel to get this paper back and see her first big red F. So, when Mr. Rathbone told the class to finish up, she was far from relieved. This test was one big disaster.

As the teacher moved between the desks collecting the test papers, people hurried to fill in their last answers. As Mr. Rathbone passed Salem, he gave him the glowing little smile teachers always give their pets. Salem had impressed him so much the other day with that stupid essay he'd written about how the stock market crash of 1929 had affected common house pets. *Well,* Sabrina thought, *when I get through with Salem's test, he'll be in the doghouse!*

Mr. Rathbone laid the quizzes in a pile on the one clear space on his book-strewn desk. Sabrina started to point. Then she stopped. It wasn't fair, really. If Salem had done great on the test, he deserved it. Changing someone's answers to make them fail was almost as bad as cheating yourself . . .

Salem leaned over his desk toward Sabrina. "So . . . how do you think you did?" he whispered.

She made a face. "Pretty bad," she said.

He threw her a fake look of concern. "Oh well. I guess

a bad grade will be the least of your problems once the Witches' Council gets done with you, huh?"

Sabrina saw red. Ooooh! Fair or not fair, that creep was going to pay! She pointed and this time she didn't stop herself. She whispered softly, *"Abracadabra, abracadibberish. Make Salem's answers turn into gibberish."* Somewhere in the pile of tests, the letters on Salem's paper transformed. In the space where it asked who the president and vice president were, it no longer said "Herbert C. Hoover and Charles Curtis." Instead, it said, "Salem Saberhagen and Libby Chessler." The president's five responses to the crash included "threw a pizza party" and "went to the mall to score some babes."

Sabrina peeked over at Salem. He was leaning back in his chair, his legs outstretched, looking as though he'd just taken a vacation in the Caribbean rather than one of Mr. Rathbone's killer quizzes. Poor Salem. He had no idea what was about to hit him. Then, just for extra credit, Sabrina pointed again. Randy Johnson's paper transformed, too. She wondered what he'd do to Salem when he got every answer he'd copied wrong!

Sabrina watched as Salem tossed a few typed sheets of paper onto Ms. Quick's desk in the office of *The Westbridge Lantern*, the school newspaper. "Here it is. All done. My article on the health hazards of asbestos in the Westbridge High building," he said.

Ms. Quick looked up for a moment, then went back to line editing an article. "Terrific. I'm really looking forward to running that on the front page," she said.

Sabrina pointed.

"But I'm afraid I can't," Ms. Quick went on. "The cheerleading squad just came in fourth in the districtwide competition. A story that big's got to go on page one. And since the rest of the issue is already laid out, we're canning your story." She picked up Salem's work and tossed it in the garbage. Then, she did a double take, staring at the tossed paper. "I wonder why I said that?" she murmured to herself. Sabrina pointed again. She shrugged and went back to her work.

"What?" Salem gasped. "That's crazy! I worked really hard on this article. And you can't really mean that cheerleaders are more important than the health of the entire student body." He bent down and rescued his article from the garbage can, wiping off unseen bits of dirt with his fingers.

Ms. Quick looked up at Salem as if he were out of his mind. "What planet are you from? The cheerleaders are *always* more important than the rest of the student body." A strange look passed over her face. "Now that's not really true," she mumbled. Sabrina pointed and she forgot what she was thinking.

"But . . . but . . . but the cheerleaders are affected by the asbestos, too," Salem said lamely, trying any argument to get his article back in the paper.

A compassionate look crossed Ms. Quick's face. Sabrina pointed and the expression slid away. Ms. Quick didn't even look up at him now. She just remained bent over his papers, spreading red marks over the article with her pen. "Sorry," she said, not sounding sorry at all.

Sabrina watched Salem redden, though whether it

was from embarrassment or anger she didn't know. He stared at Ms. Quick for a few seconds. Then, he turned around and stormed out of the room, slamming the door behind him.

Score two for me, she thought. A little more frustration like that and Salem would be sharpening his claws again in no time.

Skweeee . . . skwaaaaaa. The public address system shrieking to life for what felt like the hundredth time that day.

"Attention, students!" Mr. Kraft's voice boomed through the hallways and classrooms, interrupting lessons and daydreams alike. "Seeing as the loud speakers are working so beautifully, as you all know so well already, I thought I would take this moment to inform you of some of the school district's lesser known rules. You may not bring your pet guinea pig to school on Mondays and Thursdays. You may not stick sugarless chewing gum to the underside of your desk. Only students with brown socks may be excused from gym class." He giggled. Ever since Salem had cleaned the speakers, he'd been on even more of a power trip than usual, making announcements every three seconds about nothing whatever of importance.

Sitting next to Sabrina in English, Gordie put his fingers in his ears as if to shake out the sound of Mr. Kraft's voice. "Who fixed those stupid speakers anyway?" he muttered.

"Salem Saberhagen!" Sabrina volunteered helpfully. Might as well start the anti-Salem buzz going right away.

"He was trying to kiss up to Mr. Kraft. Now, we're all paying for it."

"What a jerk!" Gordie said.

Sabrina smiled, but she didn't really feel very good about what she was doing. Poor Salem. Trashing his reputation was mean. But it was necessary. Gordie was only a start, though. She had to get *everyone* in Westbridge High to hate Salem. She pointed at the loudspeaker. *"Fiddledeedee, fiddledeedum. Make Mr. Kraft rat on Salem."*

Mr. Kraft's voice came screeching out of the speakers again. "One more thing," he said. "I'd like to thank Salem Saberhagen for the *terrific* job he did of cleaning out all the public address speakers. It brings me that much closer to each and every one of you."

"Does it ever!" Gordie said, sounding annoyed.

Sabrina stifled a giggle. By the end of the day, even the worst kiss-ups in the school wouldn't be talking to Salem. *Score three,* she thought. She'd be cleaning the litter box again in no time.

Salem slid his brown tray across the bars of the lunchroom counter, looking lonely and forlorn. Practically the only people talking to him were the lunchroom servers, and they weren't known for their fascinating conversation. "More mashed potatoes?" a thin woman in a hair net asked him.

"No thanks," he said.

"More chipped beef Neapolitan?"

"Yes, please." The lunch person filled up his plate.

Sabrina watched as he took his tray over to the farthest table in the lunchroom and started to eat, hunched over his food. It was a sorry sight. Salem, whom everyone had been crazy about just yesterday. Now, it was as if he had the world's worst case of fleas.

Should she relent? Sit with him? Be the bright spot in his awful day?

No, she had to be ruthless. If she weren't, he'd never want to be a cat again. Luckily, Harvey and Val had already found a table as far from Salem as possible. She walked toward them, passing torn election posters featuring Salem and Libby. Someone had gone around with a black felt tip and traced a mustache on Salem in one poster, cat ears and whiskers in another. *They're already making fun of him,* she thought sadly. Still, she knew it was a good sign.

But things had to get worse. Much as she knew it was wrong, she had to make Salem's life at Westbridge completely unbearable. She turned over her shoulder and pointed. A huge red pimple popped up on the tip of Salem's nose. Sabrina didn't even bother to check out the result of her handiwork. The thought of the embarrassment was just too awful.

Score four, she thought. Unless Salem found a really great acne medicine, he wouldn't be able to show his face at Westbridge for the rest of the week!

Chapter 9

"Okay, Sabrina! I see what you're up to! You're trying to ruin my life!" Salem yelled.

His words echoed off the tall red-brick towers of the school building. Up ahead, a few couples strolled along, engrossed in nothing but each other. They didn't even look around as Salem shouted. Beyond them, a group seemed to be heading for the football field, where the Ridgefield team had gathered for the informal game Harvey had challenged them to in the Slicery. Sabrina knew both teams were waiting for Salem, to see if he was as great an athlete as he'd made himself out to be. If he did well in this game, almost nothing she did from here on in would touch him. It was now or never. She had to make Salem wish he'd never walked on two legs.

But before they started that battle for the old pigskin, Sabrina and Salem had another battle to fight, and that was between just the two of them.

Salem was mad. But Sabrina was even madder. It was the day after the history quiz and when Mr. Rathbone had returned Salem's paper to him, boy had he lit into him. In front of the whole class.

"I expected a lot more from a student with your abilities!" he'd said. "I can understand if you didn't study. But . . . you made a joke out of the entire test!"

"What do you mean?" Salem had answered, looking shocked.

In response, Mr. Rathbone's whole face had turned a deep shade of orange and gotten as puffed up as a tomato. But he hadn't yelled even then. He'd simply said, "Stand up!" And when Salem stood, he'd said, "Read your quiz answers out loud."

Salem had looked at his paper with the gigantic F on the top. Sabrina knew she'd never forget the amazement and disbelief on his face as he read over the transformed answers on the page. Then his expression had shifted and he'd shot her a wounded, betrayed look. They both knew there was only one way the answers could have changed, and she was the cause.

But she had to hand it to him. He was smart. He'd looked at Mr. Rathbone with all the charm of John F. Kennedy on the campaign trail. "This was just a joke!" he said. "Of course I know who the President and Vice President were in 1929. And not just them." Then, he'd proceeded to rattle off the names of every President and Vice President since George Washington had been elected with John Quincy Adams.

Mr. Rathbone had been impressed. Very impressed. He hadn't even ripped up the test paper, the way he usu-

ally did when he got very, very angry. And that had totally amazed the kids. You could see their respect for Salem
rising with every compliment out of Mr. Rathbone's
mouth. Salem was the no-stick guy. He could mess up
and still not get into trouble! Her plan had totally back-
fired. She had to admit it—that cat was a hard one to
outfox.

Of course, Salem had gotten in a whole lot of trouble
later, when Randy Johnson had attacked him in the hall
after class. "You *knew* I was cheating off your paper! I
flunked—because of you!" Randy had growled just
before he had sent his right fist sailing toward Salem's
whiskerless nose.

Salem had twisted as gracefully as a cat, grabbing
Randy's arm in a ninja move and throwing him halfway
across the hall. The kids standing around watching had
loved it. Maybe they'd even forgiven him a little for
cleaning out those loudspeakers.

They'd forgiven him the rest of the way when, just at
that moment, every loudspeaker in the school had
crashed to the ground. The broken speakers had lain in
little piles of twisted metal. Salem had gotten to school
early and climbed up to every one of them a second
time, then loosened the screws that mounted them to the
ceiling. Sabrina shivered at the way the crowd had
cheered for him at that moment, at Salem's self-satisfied
smile, at the thumps on the back and high fives everyone
had given him. Whatever damage she'd done yesterday
with the thank-you from Mr. Kraft, it was completely
erased.

Then, Mr. Kraft himself had come storming into the

hallway. First, he'd sadly surveyed his broken speakers. Then, he'd turned on the students gathered in the little group around Salem. "Everyone gets detention!" he'd screamed.

"But Mr. Kraft . . ." someone had started to protest in a small voice. "We didn't do anything."

"Everyone!" Mr. Kraft had insisted. He'd been so furious about his speakers, he would have given detention to the entire world, if he'd had the power. "And *you!*" He had turned to Salem, glaring at him. "You aren't even a student here, but I'm giving you detention anyway! Double detention. Triple detention. In fact, you'll be in detention for the rest of your life!"

Salem had just smiled. Sabrina had heard him murmur something under his breath. He'd said, "Just so long as I don't have to do it with four legs and a tail."

That day, there'd been so many kids in detention, it had almost seemed like a party. Harvey had passed around a huge bag of potato chips and Randy had bought everyone sodas from the vending machine. Even Ms. Quick, the teacher in charge, hadn't taken it seriously. "You know, we teachers hate detention as much as you do," she'd admitted. "It means we have to stay late, too." They'd all ended up having a massive conversation about whether or not pop music had the power to save the world.

Of course, Sabrina and Salem had spent detention glaring at each other. Afterwards, he'd confronted her as they headed toward the football field.

"You're trying to ruin my life!" he shouted again.

Sabrina looked at him sadly. "Yes. I am," she admitted, not feeling very good about the truth. She knew how hard it was to be a teenager, even when you didn't have someone actively trying to mess things up for you.

He stared at her with those big goldish-green eyes, wringing out every last bit of guilt her heart could manufacture. She felt exactly the way she did when he'd been a cat, begging for a bite of her tuna-fish sandwich. "But why? Why?" he asked her.

She stared at her feet, kicking at the grass as they walked. "Because . . . you're ruining mine! And you don't even care!"

As they left the school building behind and pushed through the low bushes that separated the football field from the rest of the school grounds, Salem was quiet, as if he were thinking about what Sabrina had said. Then he answered, "You're right. I don't care!"

Sabrina groaned. The guilt evaporated. She was going to get that cat if it was the last thing she did!

They ducked through the last of the bushes and onto the football field. On the other side, the rest of the kids were starting to gather. The Westbridge guys were doing warm-up stretches on the ground or throwing some practice passes. The Ridgefield guys were doing calisthenics in their burgundy and black uniforms. There was an older guy with a potbelly haranguing them from the sidelines. They'd brought their coach with them, Sabrina realized in amazement. The spectators had already staked out places on the bleachers. Libby and the cheerleaders had shown up and were waving around their green and white pom-poms. Harvey saw Sabrina and

Salem and waved them over with a friendly motion of his arm.

"Wow. Looks like this not-so-friendly little game has turned into a big deal," Sabrina commented as they walked toward Harvey.

Salem grinned, looking self-satisfied. "Yeah, it did. See, Coach saw a lot of talent in me and wanted to see how I'd do in a game. And the Ridgefield coach heard about me and wanted to check me out too, see what kind of competition his guys will be up against."

"But you're not even officially a student at West-bridge!" Sabrina said.

"If I score enough points during this game, I will be," Salem commented simply.

Sabrina squinted against the sun. She could just make out the coach's figure, seated midway up the bleachers with the smaller figure of his assistant sitting next to him. He had on a baseball cap and he was sucking down a can of soda. "It's not fair!" she said. "If he knew you're really a cat, he'd never tap you for the team."

Salem just shrugged. "Look, you can moan all you want, but you better get used to me. Because I'm here to stay!"

Sabrina scowled. "No way!"

"Way."

Sabrina heaved a huge sigh of frustration. "Salem! I know you're really smart. But do you truly think you can beat my magic? I mean, every single thing you do, I can turn it into a total disaster—just by pointing." She looked around to see if anyone was looking. Harvey was busy giving directions to his teammates.

Libby and the cheerleaders were in the middle of a big splits-and-cartwheels number that included the shout, "We're number four!" Val was already comfortably settled in the bleachers, waving a handmade sign that said, "Westbridge High loves Salem!" The spectators chatted among themselves. No one was paying any attention to her and Salem. So she pointed. His nose turned purple.

"Hey!" he exclaimed, peering at himself cross-eyed.

Sabrina giggled, pointed again and his nose returned to normal. "See what I mean? I'll always win."

Salem glared, but he didn't seem at all worried. "That's what you think! Look what you tried with Mr. Rathbone's test. And did it work? No! He's even crazier about me than he was before. And the kids think I can get away with anything, which is going to count big when those elections for class president come around."

"What about the newspaper story?" she asked. "Weren't you the teensiest bit disappointed when it got pulled?"

Salem grinned as widely as the cat who ate the canary. "Who do you think is covering the cheerleading competition?" he asked wickedly.

Sabrina stared at him. "No! Not you!"

Salem nodded and did a little jig across the football field. "Sure! After all, it *is* the hottest story to hit Westbridge High. And who could cover it better than the school's future number-one reporter?"

"But I planned to cover that!" Sabrina complained. As stupid as the story was, she'd do it if it meant getting an article on the front page.

"*Planned* is the operative word here," Salem practically crowed. "See, I went to Mr. Kraft and asked him to get Ms. Quick to let me write the story. At first, he said no because he blamed me for messing up all those speakers. But then I explained to him that I'd done it for his own good."

Sabrina crossed her arms over her chest, waiting for the impossible explanation to come out of Salem's mouth. "For his own good? Now how did you convince him of that?"

Salem grinned. "I said that I was shocked, shocked to see what a crummy old system the school district was making him use. I said I knew the district would never replace it as long as it still worked, even really badly. But, now that it's all in pieces, well, they'll have to get him a state-of-the-art system." He laughed evilly. "Actually, it was all very easy!"

"Amazing!" Sabrina said, feeling a bit of admiration for Salem herself now.

"And he . . . well, you're not going to believe this, Sabrina, but he actually apologized."

She probably shouldn't have believed it . . . but she was beginning to think Salem could do just about anything.

He didn't say anything more, but from the tremendous grin on his face and the way he was practically bouncing toward Harvey and the team, Sabrina knew he wasn't worried about her magic one bit. She thought about it. He was right. No matter how much she'd pointed, she hadn't accomplished anything. In fact, Salem seemed more loved by everyone at Westbridge High now than ever before. Salem's life as a teenager without magic was better than Sabrina's was with it!

Sabrina studied Salem's figure as he sauntered over the field. He looked happy, relaxed. There hadn't been even any sign of the pimple she'd popped onto his face the day before. Either he had found the most powerful zit medicine known to humankind or acne just didn't affect cats. What was the secret of his power? Her aunts had called it charisma, that special ingredient that just made everything he touched turn to gold.

Salem slowed down now, holding her with an intent gaze. "Listen," he said. "I take back everything I said before."

"You do?" Sabrina said. Now she felt really bad. Salem was apologizing. After everything she'd done to him.

"Yeah. I don't care if you try to ruin my life. In fact, this is a challenge. Just see if you can!" Then he ran off across the football field.

"Argggh!" Sabrina groaned. Her finger was itching to point. But there were too many people watching now. Besides, she was beginning to think that Salem was charmed—every bad spell she could think of flipped around and somehow ended up helping him.

She walked toward the bleachers, feeling awful. "Hey, over here!" Val waved to her. But Sabrina just shook her head and scooted behind the bleachers. She had to be someplace where she could throw spells without worrying about half the school seeing her. She sat down, folding her legs beneath her, trying to avoid the muddiest ground. She could barely see between the legs of the spectators as the guys drew together for the first play.

She could hear the cheerleaders chanting like crazy. "Westbridge rocks and Ridgefield's a zero! Salem Saberhagen, you're our hero!"

Sabrina caught just a glimpse of Salem's running form as the ball arched into the blue, cloudless sky. She pointed.

But it was just so hard to aim between the slats of the bleachers. And besides, Salem was fast. By the time the spell traveled over the field, he was somewhere else. It hit one of the guys from the other team instead. His shoe magically untied. He tripped over the dangling lace and fell right on his face in the mud.

Now Salem had a clear field halfway to the end zone. The pass flew through the air, just out of reach of his outstretched arms. But he leaped like a cat, twisted in midair, and landed the ball right in the palms of his hands. He hugged it to himself before he'd even landed, then took off down the field faster than Morris the cat trying to outrun Lassie. Eventually, a couple of the guys from the other team managed to tackle him, but only after he'd made some major footage.

The crowd went wild. "Way to go, Salem!" she heard someone up in the bleachers shouting.

"Kill 'em, Saberhagen!" someone else yelled.

"Salem, you're the best!" This last Sabrina recognized as Val's voice.

"Darn it!" Sabrina murmured.

But she kept trying. Next time they started a play, she pointed before Salem had a chance to start running. Once again, a Ridgefield guy ran in the way. "Ooof," he said as he slid on a banana peel that just happened to appear out of nowhere on the field. Salem got the ball again. And, this time, he scored.

It went on like that for the whole first half. Every time the ball got close to Salem, Sabrina threw a spell. And every time, one of the guys on the other team managed to get in the way. Then he'd be the one to blow a play or miss a tackle.

Meanwhile, Salem wracked up play after fabulous play. The crowd had taken to shouting out the score every time Westbridge made a touchdown. By the time Sabrina decided to call it quits and give up, they were ahead by 36 points. Above her, she could hear the spectators *ooh*ing and *ahh*ing. She couldn't stand it another second. She slipped the straps of her knapsack onto her back and quietly pointed herself home.

It was just so horrible. Salem wasn't the teen failure around here, Sabrina decided . . . she was!

Chapter 10

*S*abrina popped into her bedroom, dropped her knapsack onto the bed, and sank down next to it. The place was a mess—CDs spread all over her desk, the bedspread in a crumpled mess on the floor, Salem's dirty gym shorts and socks hanging off the big wooden headboard of her bed, a half-eaten tuna-fish sandwich sitting on a plate on top of the stereo.

As extra punishment—as if just having Salem around weren't enough—her aunts were forcing her to share her room with him instead of putting him in the guest room. Salem refused to put anything away since all Sabrina had to do was point it into place. At first, he'd slept on the floor in a sleeping bag. But he'd complained so much that she'd finally given up her bed and taken the sleeping bag herself. At least she got *a little* sleep that way.

She got up and shoved Salem's smelly laundry into the closet. On top of the pile of dirty clothes lay the jeweled book her father had given her. Dad. Suddenly, Sabrina ached for some good, old-fashioned fatherly advice. Words of wisdom that would help her get through this crazy situation. Her father would make it all turn out okay. That was what fathers were for, wasn't it?

She sat down cross-legged by the open door of the closet, propping the book up in her lap. She flipped to her father's page. He smiled out at her blankly for a moment. His nose looked a little bruised and swollen. The borders of the photo shimmered and he came to life.

"Sabrina!" he said.

"Hi, Dad," she said. "What happened to you?" She indicated his nose.

Her father looked annoyed now. "Oh, it's that young warlock you've been spending time with—the one with the black hair and goldish-green eyes. Yesterday, he was snooping around here and he came across me. He said some very rude things. Then he slammed the book right in my face." He rubbed his nose as if it hurt. "Sabrina, I am not pleased with the kind of company you're keeping."

"I'm not either, Dad," she said. She felt like crying.

"This warlock's bad news," her father said. "And the sooner you get him out of your life altogether, the better."

"I know, I know," Sabrina said. "It's just that . . . well, I don't know how to do it."

Sabrina's father sighed and shook his head. "Oh honey, you can't worry about his feelings. Just tell him it's over. He'll be hurt at first, but he'll get over it."

"No, Dad. It's not like that. We're just friends!" Sabrina was horrified. It was bad enough having to share her room with Salem. But for her father to think they were romantically involved . . . *yuck!*

Her father winked. "Sabrina, Sabrina. You're a teenager now. We can be honest with each other about these things. I know how things are between young people. After all, I was a young warlock once myself."

"Yeah, about five hundred years ago," Sabrina murmured.

"What's that? My hearing's not as good as it used to be."

"Oh, Dad!" It was useless. As much as he loved her, he just wasn't going to be any help. "Look, I'll get back to you on this," she said. *If I'm still in human form once the Witches' Council gets done with me.* She started to flip the book closed.

"No, Sabrina, no! Don't slam it!"

Sabrina caught the cover at the last moment. Then, very, very gently, she laid it against the pages.

Feeling miserable, Sabrina popped herself into the kitchen and collapsed into a chair. She zapped herself a glass of milk and a large plate of double-chocolate fudge 'n' chip cookies. She'd just stay here for a while. Maybe she'd stay here forever!

Out in the living room, she could hear Aunt Hilda and Drell arguing. "I can't wait to lose that extra 210 pounds that just seems to have dropped in on us," Aunt Hilda said. Sabrina could imagine her glaring in Drell's direction.

"Hey, it's Sabrina's fault that I'm here at all!"

"What do you mean? She didn't cause the inter-realm storm. That was an act of nature!"

Sabrina reached for a cookie and tried not to listen.

"Ugh. I don't know how much more of this I can take!" she moaned to no one in particular. She stuffed a cookie into her mouth, then another and another after that.

The eyes of the portrait of Aunt Louisa flicked down to her. "Oh, look at you! Feeling sorry for yourself and stuffing your face!" she said.

Sabrina looked up tiredly. "Hi, Aunt Louisa."

The portrait just glowered. "Don't try to get my sympathy. You don't know how good you've got it. At least you get to bury your troubles in chocolate. Not me—ever since I got two-dimensional, my digestion just hasn't been right!"

"I know, I know, Aunt Louisa," Sabrina said.

Aunt Louisa rattled on. "You get to go to school. Me, I've got nothing to do but hang around all day long, listening to them bicker." She nodded with her chin toward the living room, where Aunt Hilda and Drell continued to argue. "They're driving me crazy!"

Sabrina groaned. "And Salem's at school, driving *me* crazy. It's like he's got nine lives as a teenager. No matter what I do, I just can't seem to embarrass him."

"Well you better think of a way. Because when the Witches' Council gets done with you and your aunts, someone else will move into this house and probably dump all the old furniture down in the basement. And me along with it. And I refuse, absolutely refuse, to spend the next fifty years turned to face the wall!"

It was so hopeless. Even Aunt Louisa didn't understand what she was going through. It was hard, really hard, being a teenage witch. Maybe she was the one who ought to start wishing she were a cat.

Sabrina dragged herself exhaustedly to the toaster and programmed it to spring a weather report. She must have done it a trillion times since Drell had blown into town. Aunt Zelda had finally told her she was going to break the toaster after she'd checked the weather for the dozenth time in an hour. So far, she'd been lucky. The storm was holding. She remembered how Drell had said inter-realm storms could last ages, even years. Maybe by the time it was over, she'd already have graduated high school, moved away, and gone to college. Maybe Drell would just forget about her. It wasn't very likely, but it was possible.

The toaster popped up the weather report. Sabrina retrieved it and began to read. *"Sorry all you air surfers, but we're in for yet another crummy weekend. Rain, wind, and more bad weather from that inter-realm hurricane."*

"Whew!" Sabrina whistled in relief. At least there was one way that her luck was holding out. She kept reading.

"But don't you worry. You'll have your air boards strapped to your feet by Monday. The five-day forecast shows the storm clearing. Get ready for some heavy inter-realm travel—starting first thing next week!"

"Darn!" Sabrina exclaimed. Within a few days, Drell would be back in the Other Realm, powers restored and all, blabbing his mouth off about Salem to every witch on the Council. Salem just *had* to be tired of being a teenager by then. She had one weekend, just one weekend to make him wish he'd never given up his front paws.

"Well, what are you going to do?" Aunt Louisa asked. "You ought to be out there turning Salem back into a cat.

Instead, all you're doing is transforming yourself into a blimp." She glanced down at the fast disappearing plate of cookies.

"But Aunt Louisa . . ."

"Don't 'Aunt Louisa' me," Aunt Louisa interrupted. "Self-pity never got anyone anywhere."

Sabrina thought about it. She didn't really believe she could do too much to Salem. He just seemed to turn every curve she pitched him into a home run. But if she tried really hard, even if she failed, maybe she could score enough points with the Witches' Council so that they'd be lenient with her and her aunts. No, she couldn't just let Salem win without a fight.

"Okay, you're right," Sabrina said to Aunt Louisa. "I can't give up."

"That's my girl!" Aunt Louisa said proudly.

"I'll try," Sabrina said. "I may not succeed, but at least I'll try." She stuffed a few cookies into her pocket. Then she pointed herself back out to the football field. She was going to ruin Salem's game if it was the last thing she did.

Chapter 11

Sabrina was just in time to watch the football sail through the air and land with a *thunk* in Salem's waiting arms. He ran and ran, with Elbert James, the fastest guy on the Ridgefield team, close on his heels. He laughed and smiled as he ran as if he was sure Elbert would never catch him. But Salem was too self-assured. Elbert tackled him just a few feet from the end zone.

"Don't worry! We'll score in the next down!" Salem shouted as he got up, brushing some mud and grass off his uniform. The crowd went wild, shouting and screaming and stomping deafeningly on the bleachers above where Sabrina hid.

"All right, Salem!" Sabrina heard Coach shouting from the bleachers. "You're my newest star!"

No! Sabrina thought miserably. *If he's really that good, Westbridge must be so far ahead by now, not even my magic can help Ridgefield catch up.* She tried to peek through the slats of the bleachers and get a look at the scoreboard, but somebody's feet were in the way.

"Wow! Close game," commented the person belonging to the feet. "Ridgefield really picked up in the second half. We're going to have to work hard to beat them now."

"Yeah! It's incredible how they caught up and tied us."

What? Sabrina thought. She dodged under the bleachers until she found an opening between someone's smelly sneakers and somebody else's empty soda can. When she got a glance at the scoreboard, she broke into a grin. *Home Team, 48,* it said. *Visitors, 48.* They were tied! But there were also just a few seconds left on the clock.

Wow! Sabrina thought. Without her meddling, Ridgefield had played so well they'd caught up with Westbridge. If she hadn't thrown all those spells and ruined their game in the first half, they would have won! She could have kicked herself. Salem didn't need her help to lose. And by trying to make him fail, she'd accidentally made him win!

But luckily, she'd gotten back in time. She still had a chance to lose the game for Westbridge—and make it look like it was Salem's fault! One last chance, one last play, and then the clock would run out on this friendly little game of killer football.

She had to calm herself down, take a moment and get focused. What she needed was three minutes of time out! *"Bats and balls and things that roll. Give me my remote control!"* Sabrina whispered. She pointed and a small black box appeared in her hand. She pushed the stop button. Salem and the Westbridge team froze on the field in the middle of their victory dance. The Ridgefield athletes remained stuck in slumpy poses of defeat. Everyone in the bleachers was paralyzed, their arms raised in victory, their mouths open in silent cheers. Coach was stuck a few inches off the ground in the middle of a triumphant jump. In an instant, everything was blissfully silent. Even the birds had stopped chirping.

Whew, Sabrina thought. She didn't have the powers to actually rewind time, but at least she could pause it for a few moments, catch her breath, and prepare for the difficult spell she'd have to cast in the next few moments. She closed her eyes, clearing her mind of all unnecessary thoughts.

When she opened them again, she was ready. She hit the play button and everyone started moving, jumping, shouting again. Just to be on the safe side, she pushed the slow-motion button. That way, when Salem started to run, she wouldn't miss him and hit a Ridgefield guy, the way she had earlier in the game.

She watched from underneath the bleachers as the players slowly, slowly, took to the field again. They slowly, slowly got into formation and began the final play of the game. The quarterback tossed the ball to Harvey who slowly, slowly raised his arm and sent the ball spiraling in a high arc over the football field.

Slowly, slowly, the ball went sailing straight toward Salem's waiting arms. All around him, guys from the opposite team were jockeying for the tackle. "I ... have ... it ..." Salem yelled, but because of the slow motion, his voice sounded as though it were coming from the bottom of a barrel. He had caught the last pass, but if he dropped this one . . . well, everyone knew you were only as good as your last victory—or defeat.

The ball settled comfortably into Salem's palms. That's when Sabrina pointed. *"Cats and bats and things that mutter. Make Salem's fingers just like butter,"* she whispered. And because everything was moving so slowly, she was able to aim perfectly. She hit Salem right in the chest.

"Awww!" Salem groaned as the ball magically bounced off his fingers and back into the air. Ridgefield's Elbert James grabbed it before it hit the ground and started running, slowly, slowly. Salem ran after him, but Sabrina pointed again and a bunny rabbit appeared on the sidelines. The cat in him came out. He went after the rabbit, which luckily managed to hop off before he could grab it. Sabrina laughed and jumped up and down. Now she hit the fast-forward button, and Elbert zoomed faster than a cartoon character, straight down the clear field. He ran and ran and ran. No one seemed able even to get near him! Closer and closer he got to his own end zone. He crossed it! "Score!" he shouted, his voice high, like Mickey Mouse's, because of the speed. He tossed the ball in the air and hopped up and down—fast, like a chicken. His teammates ran to congratulate him. They looked so silly, Sabrina took pity on them and hit the normal speed button on her remote control.

"Great play!"

"You're the bomb!" Elbert's teammates said.

In the bleachers, people hissed. Ridgefield had won and Westbridge . . . they were the dogs—thank goodness.

Sabrina pointed at the remote control and it disappeared. She ducked out from under the bleachers and stepped into the sunlight, feeling as though she'd won that game herself.

She edged over toward where the coach was gathering his clipboard and duffel bag together, getting ready to leave. "That Saberhagen sure choked at the crucial moment," Sabrina heard him saying to his assistant. "Talented, but he can't come through on the big plays." Sabrina watched as he pushed himself out of his seat and turned his back on the playing field, and on Salem, too. That was the end of that. The coach would never pull strings to get Salem to play on the team now.

Sabrina turned her attention to Harvey and the players on Salem's team as they kicked across the grass, doing the loser's slouch. Salem trailed behind them. They looked so disappointed. Especially Harvey. All around them, the other team danced and whooped excitedly. "We did it!" a Ridgefield guy shouted.

"Way to go!" another guy on the winning team shouted.

Sabrina moved closer to the circle of the losing team so that she could hear everything. Harvey slapped the others on their backs. "We didn't win, but at least we tried," he said.

"Yeah. Most of us did, anyway," Randy Johnson added as Salem reached the group. One by one, the guys turned away from him. "By the way," Randy said to Salem. "We're revoking that honorary team membership!" They moved past him until there was nobody left but Harvey, who stared at Salem with hurt eyes. Disappointment oozed out of every pore of his body.

"Darn, Salem. What happened?" Sabrina heard him ask.

"I'm pretty sure I know!" Salem said, hunting Sabrina down with his eyes and accusing her with a look. "But you'd never believe it if I told you!"

Harvey sighed and shook his head. He looked disappointed and let down. "You said you'd come through for us."

As Salem listened to Harvey, his shoulders slumped. He was experiencing the agony of defeat big time now, Sabrina knew. She felt sorry for him. She knew what it was like to go to Westbridge High every day when you weren't top dog and no one looked up to you—at least no one very popular.

Harvey was still looking at Salem with those unhappy eyes. "Look," Salem said. "Can't we just forget this ever happened? Play another game tomorrow or something?"

Harvey stared at Salem as if he were crazy. "Hey, this is football we're talking about. Once you blow a pass like that one, there's no next game!"

Poor Salem! Sabrina thought, feeling guilty. Salem hadn't lost the game, she had. Still, she reminded herself, the whole point of this plan was to make Salem feel so bad that maybe he'd go home and take a nice, long catnap and think things over. It looked as though the plan was working. She just hadn't expected to feel so bad about it.

Salem kicked at the grass, staring at his feet. "I'm . . . sorry, Harvey. I didn't mean to let the team down. It's just that . . . well, it was as though someone threw a magic spell, and no matter how hard I tried, that ball was just not going to stay in my hands."

Harvey thought a moment, sighed, and nodded his head. "I know the feeling. You're just not on. It could happen to anyone."

"See? I knew you'd understand," Salem said.

Harvey nodded again. "I do. But that doesn't mean the other guys will."

"It's okay," Salem answered. "I'll have to live with it."

Harvey slapped Salem on the back. "Listen, Saberhagen, you're all right. Besides, it wasn't just you who lost this game. We all did. Let's head over to the Slicery. The other guys will be there, drowning their misery in pizza. We belong with them."

"Um . . . can we get anchovies?"

Harvey studied Salem seriously. "Yeah. Yeah, we can." He put his arm around Salem's shoulders and they headed off across the now empty field.

Sabrina stood there, staring after them in amazement. Salem had been about to throw in the towel—she had smelled the defeat on him! And then, Harvey comes along and includes him, comforts him, makes him feel like it wasn't all his fault Westbridge High had lost. Harvey, of all people!

She wondered if he'd still want to kiss her if the Witches' Council decided to turn her into a frog!

Chapter 12

☆

I'm really sorry you lost that game today," Val said, snuggling closer to Salem in the blue light of the video. Her cat, Sniffles, lay curled on the couch beside them, chin resting comfortably on both paws. Sabrina buzzed around them. Just for tonight, she'd turned herself into a fly. She needed to see what was going to happen with Salem and Val and maybe throw a couple of spells. Being a fly on the wall had been the only way she could think of to do it.

Salem shook his head, looking upset. "I really wanted Coach to see me at my best. Then I fumbled the ball . . ." He took a huge bite of his tuna-fish sandwich, as if that could chase away the depressing vision.

"I didn't mean *that* game. I meant the Foosball tournament at the Slicery after you blew the football game."

Salem groaned softly. "Oh, that. Yeah."

"And I'm really sorry about you splitting your pants

right in front of everyone and stuff. That must have been really embarrassing," she said.

"Uggggh," Salem moaned.

Sabrina pointed with one little wing. It was hard to aim with these things, but she did her best. She hit Salem right in the pants.

"Oh, uh, Salem?"

"What Val?"

"Your fly? It's open . . ."

"Oh, um, oooops," Salem said, sounding embarrassed. Sabrina could hear him adjusting his position on the couch and then a zipper going up. She tried to see what was going on, but it was awfully hard to get used to seeing through these fly eyes. She could hear everything, though, and her sense of smell was really working overtime. In the back of her mind, she wondered why the Berkheads didn't scrub out their garbage cans a little better, toss out the stale graham crackers in the closet, and get rid of that horrible pine-scented furniture polish. More importantly, she could smell the new angora sweater Val was wearing and her perfume, Puppy Love. Val must really like Salem if she'd been willing to shell out $29.95 for that stuff!

Frankly, Sabrina couldn't believe she was here at all. Practically no one at school was even talking to Salem after the football fiasco. But Val was still intent on romance. Some people were just sooooo desperate!

Well, tough luck, Val, Sabrina thought. As bad as she felt about ruining her friend's little romance with Salem, it had to be done. If Val had known the truth, she never would have kissed old cat breath in a million years. Anyway, after the stunt Sabrina had planned, Val wouldn't even be speaking to Salem, let alone trying to whisper sweet nothings in his pointy little ears.

She'd tried doing it a gentler way, she really had. Earlier in the evening, she'd molecular-transferred herself over and, with a point of her finger, she'd flattened three of the four tires on Val's parents' car. She'd figured there was no way Val and Salem could go to the movies together then.

Unfortunately, she'd forgotten about video. Val had bicycled over to the Movie Machine and rented *Return of the Cat People*. Now, instead of sitting together in a big, public movie theater, they were snuggled up on Val's couch, chowing down on popcorn and tuna-fish sandwiches, barely watching the movie at all.

Well, might as well start the fireworks, Sabrina thought. She readjusted her antennae and pointed with her wing. A strand from Val's sweater disengaged from the rest of the fabric. It edged over to Salem's finger and tied itself onto it. Now, all she had to do was wait for Val to get up and get herself a soda, or answer the phone, or go to the bathroom . . . Sabrina's plan was to *unravel* this romance for good, save Val from getting pawed by Salem and teach Salem just how awful a high school romance could turn out. Sabrina glided up to the ceiling and settled there. She folded her legs beneath her, tucked her wings around her, and waited for the fun to begin.

Val sighed and nestled closer to Salem. Sniffles got up, arched her back, then turned over and lay down on her other side. Salem kept his eyes pinned on the video. *Do something! Come on, do something!* Sabrina thought.

Val did. She reached out and ran a finger slowly down Salem's arm. Luckily, he didn't seem to notice at all. In fact, he seemed entirely wrapped up in his thoughts— and they didn't seem to be very happy thoughts, either. He heaved a huge sigh. He ate another couple of bites of his sandwich. He sighed again.

"What's the matter?" Val asked. She continued to run her finger up and down his arm.

He sighed again. "I don't know," he said. "Between yesterday and today, everything's changed. One day, I was the hero. The next, I'm a nobody. Or at least, that's how it feels to me. But . . . maybe it isn't really true?" He looked eagerly at Val as if she could reassure him.

From the ceiling, Sabrina could hear every word.

Val smiled sympathetically and angled herself into the crook of Salem's arm. "No, I'm afraid it's all too true. You wouldn't be able to live down fumbling that pass if you spent the next thousand years at Westbridge! But that's high school. Hard. Cold. Brutal." She smiled again, this time happily, and laid her head on Salem's shoulder.

Tell it like it is! Sabrina thought. Listening to Val, she almost felt like giving up, leaving Salem alone, letting him enjoy the little bit of teenage fun there was to be had. Or maybe she should just turn herself into a cat.

"But that's so unfair!" Salem said. He seemed not to notice Val's snuggling.

"Yeah, isn't it!" Val answered, blissed out.

"Mrreow," Sniffles yawned, as if agreeing with them both.

But Salem obviously wanted more than sympathy. He

wanted answers. "How can you stand it? I thought being in high school would be easy. It was the last time I did it."

"Get real!" Val said. "Everyone knows a teenager's life is a series of constant crises! Now Sniffles here, her life is easy." She reached out and patted the cat with one hand.

Super! Sabrina thought. She couldn't have asked Val to say anything more perfect if she'd written the words herself.

"I mean, all Sniffles has to do is lie around and look cute. Then, every so often, someone comes along and puts out her dinner and gives her catnip."

There was a moment of silence as Salem thought. What would he do, Sabrina wondered. Would he listen to reason? Tell Val she was so horribly right?

"Catnip," he said thoughtfully. "I could use a little of that myself right now . . ." He looked even sadder than he had when the vet had given him those big shots. "But . . ." Salem went on, "don't you think Sniffles' life is boring? I mean, if she wants to head over to the Slicery and eat an entire anchovy pizza, can she do it? If she wants to take in a movie, can she pop the video in the machine? Drive a car? Throw a football? No! She can't do any of those things."

"Hmm, I never thought of it that way," Val said.

"Of course not," Salem said bitterly. "No one ever thinks about the house pet."

"I suppose you're right."

"Life really stinks when you don't have opposable thumbs!" Salem murmured.

Val reached her hand around to Salem's dark hair and started running her fingers through it. "Maybe so. But we've got them. So who cares?" She continued to caress him, tickling the back of his neck.

For a moment, he just sat there, lost in thought, not even noticing. But as Val started to run her fingers behind his pointy ears, he woke up. "Ohh," he said. "That feels really good."

"Doesn't it!" Val replied. She leaned over, closer and closer.

She's going to kiss him! Sabrina thought, totally grossed out.

She had to stop it or she'd never forgive herself. Besides, once Salem started getting a love life, it would be ten times as hard to convince him to be a cat again. She pointed with her wing.

Achoooo! Salem sneezed, practically in Val's face. He covered his nose.

"What's the matter? I hope you're not allergic to Sniffles," Val said, concerned. Though she did back up by at least a foot.

"Nope. No chance I'm allergic to the cat," Salem said. As he lowered his hands, Sabrina pointed again. A long string of mucus hung from one of Salem's nostrils.

"Eww, gross," Val exclaimed.

Salem wiped his nose with the back of his hand.

"Eww," Val said again.

Sabrina pointed a third time.

"What's that smell?" Salem asked suddenly, his nose twitching just the way it used to when he had four legs and a tail.

"You're not going to sneeze again, are you?" Val asked, wrinkling her nose.

Salem wasn't listening. "It must be your perfume!" he said.

"Oh wow. You noticed," Val said. "You like it?"

Salem sniffed again. "It smells like . . . tuna fish!"

Val looked at him, shocked. "You mean, it's gone bad? Maybe that's why it was reduced to $4.99!" She jumped up. "I've got to wash this off."

"No! I really like the way it smells!" Salem shouted.

But Val was already heading for the bathroom.

Okay. This is it, Sabrina thought. She watched as a string of pink yarn trailed from the end of Val's sweater straight to Salem's finger, where Sabrina had tied it herself via her spell. As Val hurried out of the living room, the sweater slowly unraveled. *By the time she gets to the bathroom,* Sabrina told herself, *she'll be practically topless. And she'll blame Salem because he's holding the end of the yarn!* She almost didn't want to watch how mad Val was going to get at him. The twinge of guilt was starting to throb now.

"Yeaaaagh," came a shriek from the bathroom.

Val came streaking back into the living room. Her bare stomach was visible above the waistline of her jeans, and the bottom of her white satin bra showed just below the place where the sweater had stopped unraveling. *If she'd gone into the kitchen or up the stairs or taken out the trash, she would have lost the entire sweater,* Sabrina thought.

Salem just sat there, staring at Val, who stood with her hands crossed over her chest to hide anything embarrassing that might be showing. She glared at Salem. "Wow!" Salem said. "You changed into a new outfit!"

"You idiot! You've totally ruined my sweater!" Val shrieked. "My new sweater, which I bought on sale for $7.99!" She ran toward him as if she were going to slap his face, then remembered that she was practically half naked and stopped, hiding herself again.

"Me?" Salem said, sounding shocked.

Val stamped her food. "Don't try to act innocent. Not while you're sitting there holding the end of the yarn." She pointed at the telltale piece of pink yarn.

Salem looked down at the end of the string in his hands, then back up at Val, then at the string again. "But I didn't . . . It wasn't me who . . ." Suddenly he looked around and Sabrina knew he understood who'd tied that yarn to his finger. *Don't look up here,* she thought frantically, trying to make herself even tinier than she already was.

Val was still waiting. "So? What have you got to say for yourself?"

"Uh," Salem stalled. "I guess if I said I was trying to undress you with my eyes, you wouldn't take that as a compliment, right?"

Val's eyes bugged out in amazement. "Then you *were* trying to undress me! And you ruined this totally great new sweater to do it! Salem Saberhagen, you're a jerk!"

"It wasn't my fault!" Salem said. "I couldn't help it . . ."

Now Val sighed and shook her head. She looked at Salem with the compassion of a social worker. "Salem, you need help," she said. "Professional help."

"It's not me who needs help," he raved, still looking around the room as if seeking out Sabrina's hiding place.

"This is so sad. I liked you, Salem, I really liked you. But I think it's time for you to leave."

Salem stopped raving for a moment and looked at Val. He couldn't help but see how it must seem to her, Sabrina thought. In her eyes, only the two of them were in the room. And the yarn led directly to the guilty party.

When he was licked, he knew it. He pushed up off the couch, untied the piece of yarn from his finger, and let the end drop to the floor. "Val, I'm really sorry things turned out this way. You were really nice to me when everyone stopped talking to me and—"

Val cut him off. "Save me the sob story!" She pointed toward the door.

Salem sighed heavily. "I smell a rat," he said. "And I think her name is Sabrina!" With that, he grabbed his jacket and hotfooted it out of Val's house.

Sabrina looked for an open window and winged her way out of it. When she found herself in the cool night, she pointed at herself and became a teenager once again, then pointed again and transferred herself home. She wanted to make sure she was in human form before she ran into Salem again. With the way he must be feeling right now, if she were still a fly, he wouldn't think twice about flattening her.

Chapter 13

Of course you should go to Libby's party, Salem. She'd be soooo disappointed if you didn't," Sabrina said. She turned back to her mirror, pointing herself into platform shoes and a flower-print granny skirt that reached to her ankles. She wished she felt a little better about what she was about to do. She'd thought it would be fun to mess up Salem's life. Instead, she found herself feeling sorry for him again and again. And feeling pretty lousy about herself to boot. This was *Salem*, after all. Salem, her little kitty. Salem, whom she loved!

Salem sat on the edge of the bed, holding his head in his hands. "Why should I believe you?" he moaned miserably. "You're the one who's been messing everything up for me."

"Oh, but I wouldn't lie about this," Sabrina lied. She pointed again and appeared in a plaid, pleated miniskirt and low boots. "Look, you said it yourself. The food, the keg of root beer, the music—it's all going to be great. This is a party you just can't miss!" She pointed yet a third time and dressed herself in velvet hip-huggers and a matching jacket.

Earlier that day, Sabrina had caught Salem visiting the kittens in the pet store at the mall. He'd been feeding them kitty treats and cooing at them in baby talk. She'd known then that he was only one humiliation away from begging for his tail and claws again. She had to get him to go to Libby's party. It was the perfect opportunity to end this unhappy situation for good. If he was already the dog around Westbridge, what she planned to do to him at Libby's would make him lower than an amoeba.

"I'm not going to listen to you," Salem said, burying his head under a pillow. "I'm not that stupid."

Sabrina shrugged. "Okay." She pointed again and checked out how she looked in a simple black dress and pearls. "Then what *are* you going to do tonight? It *is* Saturday, you know. Only losers stay home on Saturdays."

She didn't really think it was true. Sometimes, her best Saturday nights were the ones she shared with a good book. But she had to make Salem feel bad—worse than he'd ever felt in his life. She pointed herself into leather pants and a pink T-shirt with a red heart in the center.

Salem peeked out from under the pillow. "Um . . . I don't know what I'm doing. What are you doing?"

She pointed and her hair looped itself into a bun. She pointed again and it was in a dozen tiny braids. "Oh, Harvey and I are going to Libby's," she said trying to sound nonchalant instead of just plain miserable and guilty.

As much as she hated the thought of it, she knew she had to do it. She could already hear Libby greeting her at the door with a pleasant, "Hi freakazoid. Who invited you?" Yup, going to Libby's would be almost as humiliating for her as it was going to be for Salem. Almost, but not quite.

"You're going?" Salem said, sounding shocked. "But you weren't even invited!"

"I'll be there as Harvey's date. And Val will be there. And the guys from the football team. *Everyone* will be there, Salem. Oh, except you, of course." She pointed her hair into one long braid, then added a reddish wash to the natural gold color.

"Of course," Salem groaned, diving under the pillow again.

Sabrina checked herself out one last time and grabbed her bag. "I'm out of here. Don't wait up for me—I think this party's going to go all night. And whatever you plan to do this evening, have a *great* time."

"Ughhhhh," Salem grunted.

As she headed out, Sabrina thought to herself, *See you at Libby's.* There was no way Salem was going to stay home now and be one of the losers who didn't have a thing to do on a Saturday night. Nope, he'd be at that party—no matter how much of a disaster he knew it was going to be.

"Salem, you freak, *what* are you *doing* here?" Libby shrieked as she answered the door.

Salem peered inside quickly, as if he were checking to make sure no one had heard. Of course, everyone had—

when Libby screeched like that, there was no way you could miss her. Sabrina watched Salem redden in embarrassment but—and she had to admire him for it—he didn't let it keep him from walking in the door. "Hi, Libby," he said. "Nice to see you."

It was pretty hard to hear over the noisy bashing of the drummer of Venus and the Fly Traps, the chattering of the other partygoers, and the sound of the root beer keg constantly whooshing soda into oversized cups. The caterers Libby's mother had hired wove in and out among the guests, offering them plates of beautiful little sandwiches. There was a huge buffet spread, too.

Sabrina didn't want to miss a word of what was coming between Libby and Salem. She pointed at herself and a tiny hearing aid appeared in her ear. It squawked for a moment and she adjusted it. "Listen," Libby was saying desperately, "you can't stay here. Everyone will think this is a party for losers."

"Well I can't leave," Salem answered. "Otherwise, everyone will know how shallow and two-faced you are."

At that moment, Sabrina wasn't sure whose side she was on. If Libby really harassed Salem, it would give him the last kick in the pants he needed to give up his heart's desire forever. But right now, she was kind of enjoying watching Salem give Libby a taste of her own medicine. She struggled to keep them in sight among the crowd of people flirting, dancing, chug-a-lugging root beer, laughing.

Libby scowled at Salem, standing there with her hands on her hips. He was right about her being two-faced. Even she couldn't deny it. "Okay, okay," she said. "Come in. But don't stay too long!"

"I guess this means I should find someone else to be my running mate for the elections, huh?" Salem said.

"You bet, freak-face!" Libby said. "And I won't need you to tutor me in chemistry, either. I'd rather fail!"

"Sounds like a plan to me!" Salem pushed past Libby, a smile pasted to his face. He was trying to put up a good front, but Sabrina could see how hard it was for him. He glanced around the crowd, looking for friends. He waved at Val, but she turned away, flinging her dark hair behind her with a hurt toss of her neck. "I am just sooo fascinated by your stamp collection," she said to the guy she was standing with. "Tell me more." She studiously avoided even looking at Salem.

Salem's face fell. Then he turned away and pushed his way through the crowd to the root beer keg. "Hey!" he called to a couple of the guys on the football team. They pretended not to hear.

Salem looked like he'd been tackled by a pro linebacker. It was awful to watch. Sabrina felt like running over to him, giving him a hug, wiping that horrible expression of rejection and shame off his face for good. But she couldn't. She had to be mean, heartless. Anything she did to lessen Salem's misery would bring her one step closer to standing before the Witches' Council.

Salem grabbed a cup and began to fill it with root beer. As he finished, he jostled into someone standing behind him. It was Harvey. Salem turned and as his and Harvey's eyes met, Sabrina saw fear in his face. She could imagine exactly how he felt—alone, embarrassed, awkward.

They stared at each other for one long moment. Then, Harvey broke into a smile. "Hey, Salem! How are you? I'm sorry about the pants yesterday, dude. Could happen to anyone—though of course, I'm glad it didn't happen to me."

Sabrina listened, feeling both proud of Harvey and annoyed at him. Of everyone in school, he was the only one who seemed not to care about all the mess-ups Salem had made in the past few days. On the other hand, if he'd known what was at stake for Sabrina, maybe he wouldn't have been quite so friendly to Salem . . .

Salem's expression shifted and he grinned. "You know, it's really great to see you. How about we get together tomorrow and throw the old pigskin around a little . . ."

"Sounds great!" Harvey said.

Darn, Sabrina thought. *I've got to knock this game out in the first play . . .*

She pointed. Salem's root beer cup went tipping, tipping . . . the soda splattered all over Harvey.

"Oh no," Salem exclaimed. He lunged for some napkins, but he slipped on the puddle of root beer. As he fell, he grabbed for the closest thing to steady himself. It was the keg. His hand hit the nozzle and root beer came shooting out in a long steady stream, aimed directly at Harvey's head. The music ground to a halt. People stopped talking in mid-sentence. Everyone stared. Then, somebody started to laugh. It took practically two whole minutes before they managed to turn the root beer off.

When it was over, Harvey looked down at Salem, still lying on the ground, then at his wet, sticky clothes. "About Sunday . . ." he said.

"I know, I know," Salem said. "You forgot your great-aunt Mamie's coming into town and you just can't make it."

"Something like that." He shook his head sadly as he moved away from Salem, leaking root beer with every step.

This has got to be it, Sabrina thought. *Salem's out of here this instant. The humiliation will be just too much.* She herself could never have stood it. She would have run out of there in a second, never to show her face at Westbridge High again.

But she had to hand it to Salem—he was persistent. He picked himself off the floor, wiped away some of the root beer, and headed for the refreshment table as if nothing at all had happened. When he got there, everyone moved away, as if being unpopular were a disease they could catch if Salem did so much as breathe near them. Sabrina couldn't believe how strong he was, just standing there by the pigs-in-a-blanket, pretending his social life wasn't over. You couldn't help but admire that in a person . . . or cat. It didn't matter which for this one moment. Sabrina simply felt unbelievably proud of him.

Libby wandered over to the refreshment table. She poked around in the bowl of chips, pretending she was just checking to make sure there were enough left rather than let on that she'd actually come over to talk to Salem. "Don't you think it's time for you to go now? Haven't you shown your freak-master face around here long enough?" As she spoke, she barely moved her mouth so that no one would see her talking to him.

Salem's shoulders slumped and he answered her so softly that Sabrina had to turn up her hearing aid to catch what he said. "Hey, you invited me here," he told Libby. "So if I'm a freak master, that means you're one, too."

Libby's face turned slightly green. "Don't you ever let anyone hear you say that."

He grinned at her, but he looked a little sick. It was totally pitiful to watch. But in this case, pity was a weakness. Sabrina had to finish Salem off, once and for all.

She started to point . . . but watching Salem's unhappy face, she couldn't do it. No, he'd been through enough. He'd always been a totally great cat. Now, he was a great teenager. And no one knew it because of everything she had done. It wasn't nice. And it wasn't fair. Sabrina grew just a little bit in that moment. What she grew was a conscience.

The more she thought about it, the more she realized how wrong she'd been. If the Witches' Council punished her, so be it! After all, they'd be punishing her for a reason. She'd been terribly careless with Drell's Heart's Desire chip. That really did make her responsible for Salem turning into human form. Whatever the Council did to her, she'd deserve it!

As Sabrina watched Salem stuffing pigs-in-a-blanket into his mouth as he talked quietly to Libby. She turned off her hearing aid. She didn't want to eavesdrop anymore. Once this conversation was over, she and Salem would get their behinds out of here. It was still early enough to rent a video. They'd go home together, have a little heart-to-heart talk, then curl up in the sofa together and just zone out. It would be fun! Just like the old days, but with Salem about 120 pounds heavier than before.

"Coming through, coming through," someone said loudly, pushing past Sabrina and jostling her out of her daydream.

It was one of the caterers, hoisting a huge platter of something over his head. Sabrina watched him ease his way through the crowd, then plunk his silver platter down in the center of the buffet table.

"What's that?" Salem said, sniffing.

Don't! Sabrina thought. Any second now and he'd start licking his paws.

Libby said, "I think it's . . ."

But Salem didn't let her finish. "It's fish!" he practically crowed.

Sabrina peered as closely as she could at the platter. Sure enough, it was filled with saltine crackers. Each one was covered with cream cheese, with an anchovy laid on top. *That ought to get him,* she thought. She watched as, without even seeming to realize it, Salem reached out and plucked an anchovy off one of the saltines. He looked as though he were hypnotized. He popped it in his mouth, and before he'd even finished chewing, he'd pulled another one off the tray. The anchovy jiggled as he moved it toward his mouth, dripping oil.

"Yuck!" Sabrina heard Libby exclaim.

Salem looked at the anchovy as if he hadn't even known it was there. He popped it in his mouth and automatically reached down for the next one. A bit of anchovy juice glistened on his chin. Libby was looking at him like he was a Martian with antennae and everything.

No, Salem, don't! Sabrina thought. She'd been trying so hard to embarrass him and here he was now, totally humiliating himself, without any help from her. She could barely stand to watch it. *I could cast a spell,* she thought. *Or try to get him alone someplace and zap us both home using molecular transference . . .*

"Coming through again!" the caterer called, hefting up an even bigger platter this time. He slid between the dancing bodies gracefully. Then, he plunked his tray down on the table, right next to the other one. Sabrina couldn't see what was on it.

Salem's nose whisked back and forth as quickly as a bee's wings. "Wh-wh-what's th-that s-smell . . . ?" he asked, almost too excited to get the words out.

"Just a little party food, freak-brain," Libby answered.

But now, Sabrina knew what was on the table. Tunafish salad! The caterer had pressed it into dainty little sandwich squares. "Salem! Control yourself!" she started to cry out.

But before she could finish, Salem had gone berserk. He pushed Libby out of the way and she fell flat on her rear. He leaped at the table, swiping at it with his hands, shoveling tuna sandwiches in his mouth with big, greedy motions. For the second time that night, the music faded into nothingness and the crowd stopped and stared.

"What's he doing?" Val gasped.

"What a pig!"

"He's weird."

No, he's just a cat, Sabrina thought. *A very normal cat who can't control himself when it comes to one thing in the world. And someone just put a whole plate of it in front of him.*

"Yum. Mmmmmmm!" Salem said, slobbering and shoving another half dozen tuna sandwiches in his mouth.

"Salem Saberhagen, you are disgusting!" Libby said, her voice ringing out over the shocked murmurs of the others.

"Yeah, gross."

"It's making me sick just to watch him!"

But even then, Salem didn't stop. He continued to grab tuna salad with his bare hands. He didn't stop until every single tuna square was gone.

And then, he did the worst thing, the thing even Sabrina herself would never have thought of. He vomited.

"Yeeachhh!"

"Revolting!"

"Grotesque!"

Salem turned then, noticing, as if for the first time, the room full of people staring at him. "Uh, it's just a little hairball, guys. No big deal." But Sabrina could see he was dying there, shivering in his sneakers.

It was horrible, awful, totally humiliating. Sabrina had hoped for just this for days. But now that it had happened . . . well, she felt like a traitor for her part in it. Poor Salem, he wouldn't be able to show his face within the county limits, let alone at school. She walked over and slipped her arm around his. "I think it's about time we headed home now, don't you?"

Salem stared for a moment at all the kids standing around watching him. Kids he'd thought were his friends. They were looking at him like a bunch of campers who'd just run into Bigfoot.

"Yeah," he said. "Yeah, I guess you're right."

Sabrina was proud of the way he walked all the way to the door with his head held high, not batting an eyelash, as if he had nothing in the world to be ashamed of. He didn't break down and howl until they were at least five blocks from Libby's house. They sat on the curb and she comforted him while he cried. Every so often, a car would zoom by, catching them in its headlights. Bit by bit, Salem's sobs tapered off. He sniffed a little. Finally, he was quiet.

When he looked at Sabrina, his eyes were glassy with tears. "I know I ought to be mad at you, but I'm not."

"You aren't?" Sabrina said, amazed.

Salem shook his head. "Nope. Because even though it was you who made all those terrible things happen to me, you didn't tell the kids how to react to them. I mean, sure, you made me miss the football pass. But the guys on the team could have been supportive. They could have said, 'Better luck next time!' "

Sabrina's eyes grew big. She couldn't believe what she was hearing. Salem didn't even seem annoyed at her. After all the spells she'd thrown at him.

"And Val could have given me the benefit of the doubt with the sweater, but did she? *Uh-uh.* And Libby could have been a little nicer at the party. I mean, we were supposed to be friends."

Upset, Sabrina bit off the tip of one of her nails. "You don't really mean all that stuff, do you?" she asked. *Don't feel guilty. Don't feel guilty,* she told herself.

Salem turned to Sabrina and held her gaze with his teary eyes. "Yeah, I really do mean it. It wasn't nice, what you did, but it wasn't nearly as bad as what the others did."

Sabrina laid a comforting hand on Salem's shoulder. "Don't take it personally. They really did like you. It's just that . . . well, teenagers can be like that."

Salem sighed heavily. "What teenagers can be is . . . awful."

They were the words Sabrina had been praying to hear. But now that Salem had said them, they didn't sound that good. Maybe they were necessary, but she wished she hadn't had to torture Salem quite so terribly in order to get him to believe them.

"But," Salem continued, "what I really wanted to say was . . . thanks for getting me out of Libby's. I know it was probably embarrassing just to be seen with me."

"It's *never* embarrassing to be seem with you, Salem," Sabrina said.

And she meant it. After everything that had happened, she was still incredibly proud of him. He'd handled every situation with cleverness and dignity . . . except maybe for the tuna-fish bender at the refreshment table. She reached out and scratched behind his ear. He perked up for a moment, then settled back into a daze.

"You've always been a good friend," Salem said.

"I'm sorry it had to be the way it was," Sabrina answered sadly.

Salem nodded. "I understand. If things had been the other way around, I would have done the same things you did." There was a moment of silence. Then he said, "Do you think we could stop off at the supermarket before we go home?"

Sabrina shrugged. "I guess so. What do you want to get?"

"Well I . . . uh . . . I wanted to stock up on some Pretty Kitty Treats."

Sabrina knew for sure she'd won then. "No problem," she answered gently. She hadn't enjoyed being mean to Salem. She was glad it was finally over.

Chapter 14

☆

☆

Salem prowled around Sabrina's room, pacing up one way and down the other. She could almost picture his tail whisking back and forth already. Salem stopped pacing for a moment.

"Okay, I'm ready," he announced. "I'll miss those opposable thumbs but . . . it will be really nice to have my claws back." He looked at Sabrina and nodded. "Yeah," he said. "Yeah, I'm ready." He went over to the edge of the bed, sat down, waiting quietly, watching Sabrina with his big, goldish-green eyes.

Sabrina went to her closet and got out the special outfit she always wore for when she had to cast a spell that was *really* important. Black designer jeans, a black velvet top, and her tall, pointy witch's hat. She'd been pleased the day she'd realized those drab old gowns weren't really necessary, that it was perfectly acceptable to dress in something stylish—as long as it was black.

126

The hat, of course, was kind of old-fashioned, so she didn't usually use it for casting spells, but somehow, this situation seemed to need a little extra pomp and ceremony. She pressed the hat onto her head, then closed her eyes and focused hard. If she'd ever wanted to cast the perfect spell, she did now. Her entire future depended on it. Besides, Salem deserved a Grade A, top-quality spell. He'd gone through enough for it.

She began. *"Life's too hard at Westbridge High . . ."*

But before she could finish saying the words that would transform Salem back into a cat, there was a flash of light and a pouf of smoke. Salem's desire to be a cat was even stronger than her spell. He was actually transforming himself back into feline form just by the force of his own mind! When the smoke cleared, Salem the boy was gone. In his place was a small black cat, who sat on the bed licking his fur.

Sabrina stared at him for a moment, almost unable to believe her eyes. It was over! Salem was back to normal!

But beneath the relief, there was also a tinge of sadness. She'd miss seeing Salem at school. He'd been so much fun—even when she'd been *really* mad at him. More than that, Sabrina felt sorry for Salem. It must be hard to give up your heart's desire, no matter how much of a pain in the neck it turned out to be.

"Better?" she asked, scratching him behind the ears.

"Much," he said, purring deeply. "Just don't tell anyone over at the Warlocks' Club. If they ever found out I *chose* to be a cat, they'd revoke my membership for good."

"I didn't know they accepted cats as members."

"As long as you pay your dues . . ." He hung his head now, looking at her sheepishly, begging her with his eyes. "Say you won't tell, Sabrina. Please?"

Sabrina continued to scratch. "Don't worry, Salem. You can trust me." They looked at each other. Despite everything that had happened between them recently, they both knew it was true. For the first time since the inter-realm hurricane had blown Drell into the house, they shared a moment of peace.

But the peace didn't last long. *Bam, bam, bam.* Someone pounded on Sabrina's door. "Sabrinaaaaa. Are you in there?" Drell singsonged. Sabrina didn't like it. He sounded far too happy . . . which probably meant trouble for her.

Before she could say "Come in," or "Go away!" Drell flung the door open and burst into the room. He was wearing a black suit and a pair of dress shoes. His hair was neatly combed. No piercings, no tattoos. He must have dressed himself, for once. "The inter-realm hurricane is over!" he announced. "My powers are back. And now . . . the Witches' Council is going to hear about *everything!*" He started to point.

"Wait, wait!" Sabrina cried. She held up one hand as if it could ward off every horrible thing Drell had ever wished on her. "I cleared up the problem with Salem. Don't I get any points for that?"

Drell scratched his chin and studied Salem who, playing along perfectly, cocked his head to one side, opened his goldish-green eyes wide, and looked the picture of innocence. "Yes, I guess you do," Drell said.

"So what is it exactly that you want the Witches' Council to punish me for?"

Drell thought for a moment. Then a furious expression crossed his face. "For all those *ridiculous* outfits you put me in. In fact, I'm in the mood for instant gratification. Let me cast a little spell myself!" He pointed.

"No! Don't!" Sabrina screamed, but it was too late.

In the instant before the spell hit her, she experienced a wave of terror. After everything she'd done, after trying so hard . . . she was still going to end up as an insect or a worm or something really small and distasteful. She felt the magic of the spell swirling around her, as if she'd just dived into a huge glass of club soda.

Then it was over. The last bubbles of the spell burst or floated away. Sabrina tried to wiggle her wings but . . . there didn't seem to be any. *Oh no,* she thought, *he's turned me into an ant.* But then she twiddled her fingers. They were still there.

"That ought to teach you!" Drell shouted. Then, he stormed out of the room and slammed into the portal to the Other Realm through the linen closet. From underneath the door, a flash of lightning glared and a deafening roar ferried Drell back to the Other Realm.

"Good riddance!" Sabrina said.

"You can say that again," Salem purred. "But . . . uh . . . you may not be very happy with the spell he zapped on you." He looked at Sabrina, made a face, then snickered.

"What? What?" she asked, too terrified to guess. Then she caught sight of herself in her full-length mirror. "Oh the horror. The horror!" she gasped as she realized what Drell had done to her.

He'd pointed her into a *Little House on the Prairie* dress, complete with a high ruffled collar and with about as much shape as a potato sack. On her feet were a pair of drippy Maryjane shoes. Her hair was in pigtails and tied with two drab brown ribbons. If anyone ever saw her looking like this, she'd die of embarrassment.

"It's certainly not one of your best looks," Salem agreed.

Sabrina turned away from her reflection in disgust and humiliation and sank down on the bed next to Salem, burying her head in her hands. "You know," she said to him, "you were right. Being a teenager can be hard."

She started to point herself out of the clothes. *But then again, being a cat just might be worse . . .* she thought. At the last moment, she turned her finger toward Salem. A large cat bowl filled with tuna fish appeared on the floor in front of him.

"Thanks, Sabrina. I needed that," he said, hopping off the bed. Then, he went for the tuna fish the way . . . well, exactly the way a cat would.

About the Author

Margot Batrae is the author of twenty-one books for young readers, including mysteries, romances, soap operas, and adventure stories. She wrote her first novel at the age of twenty-three. Four of her books have been on bestseller lists. She also writes for adults and teaches fiction writing.

Margot loved books about witchcraft, magic, and enchanted beings when she was a child and she's very glad to be writing about a witch now—especially one with as good a wardrobe as Sabrina! Margot lives in New York City, where she was born and raised. She has studied ballet for many years and used to be a modern dancer.

Margot's first cat, Rosie, was a very dark calico who had been abandoned at the vet's office at the age of seventeen (over one hundred in human years). "I'd never had a cat before," Margot says, "but I knew this one was special, and she really needed me. I just had to take her home." Rosie died two years later, after lots of love and attention. Today, Margot has two cats. Snaporaz, a black tuxedo cat, belonged to a friend who moved away. She found Tigerlily, a super-friendly, mostly white calico, living on the streets of New York. They are best pals. Margot says, "I didn't get my first pet until I was over thirty years old. Now, I wouldn't be without one!"

Let Sabrina cast a spell on you in her next magical book . . .

#27 Haunts in the House

Halloween's coming up and what better way to celebrate
than with a haunted-house fundraising event. Everyone in
Westbridge pitches in including . . . a hobgoblin! Hobgoblin's
are great guys to have arorund — they protect your house
and like nothing better than helping out in any way they
can. But, don't upset them because then . . . they turn
nasty! Which is just what Sabrina discovers when Salem
goes out of his way to ruin the Hobgoblin's day.

Instead of helping, the hobgoblin reeks havoc and causes
chaos galore. And, according to Sabrina's aunts, there
isn't the witch born that can match a hobgoblin in sheer
magical fury. Gulp. Looks like this could be the scariest
Halloween ever!

Gaze in to the future and see what wonders lie in store for
Sabrina, The Teenage Witch

#28 Up, Up and Away

Sabrina and her three mortal friends, Harvey, Valerie and
Libby have blown their science project sky high! They've got
one week to re-do their pathetic project but they're feeling
less than enthusiastic! Luckily for them, before they can get
started, Sabrina finds a puzzle with a spell that transports
them to Paris in 1783. Things go from bad to worse when
the four friends find themselves captive at the hands of a
couple of crazy French hot-air balloonists!

They're determined to break out and it looks like the only
way is up . . . and down – literally – as they do a crash
course in ballooning and learn plenty about science along
the way!

Nancy Drew™

Another famous detective from Pocket Books

Runaway Bride

False Pretences

Out of Bounds

Making Waves

Designs in Evil

Flirting with Danger

Fatal Attraction

Till Death Do Us Part